0115
9396964

MOCKERY GAP

Mockery Gap

T. F. POWYS

faber and faber

This edition first published in 2011
by Faber and Faber Ltd
Bloomsbury House, 74–77 Great Russell Street
London WC1B 3DA

Printed by CPI Antony Rowe, Eastbourne

A CIP record for this book is available from the British Library

ISBN 978-0-571-27893-0

CONTENTS

MOCKERY GAP

Chapter 1

THE SEA

ALTHOUGH the sea was its near neighbour, Mockery Gap wasn't proud of its presence. In the direction where the sea was, the people felt that instead of all that unnecessary water there might have been a town with shops, green fields where hay could be made in the summer, or at least a heath where cows could get a modest living and where donkeys could be happy.

Mockery Gap wasn't exactly beside the sea, though near to it. The sea was separated from the village by two or three wide meadows. Only one man, amongst the folk of Mockery who milked the cows, fed the ducks, scolded the children, told pretty tales of scandal about one another, and listened to the preaching of Mr. Pattimore against the wickedness that all young women are so fond of, had ever been known to be brave enough to try to make friends with the sea.

This brave man was Mr. Dobbin.

It is sometimes said that people who are very contrary to one another can get on very well together. But though Mr. Dobbin was very different from the sea, he could never get on with it. The sea wasn't a monkey, and it couldn't be petted into friendship. Mr.

Dobbin was inclined to ponder about things, the inclination of his mind was naturally towards melancholy, and any kind of noise or rudeness made Mr. Dobbin shiver. Mr. Dobbin found that the sea was a great deal too happy for him as well as too noisy.

One day in conversation he asked Mr. Caddy what he ought to do to quiet the sea, so that he shouldn't always be losing his lobster-pots. Mr. Caddy, who of all the Mockery people was supposed to understand more about the sea than any one else, replied that the best thing Mr. Dobbin could do was to let the sea alone.

'Don't touch it,' said Mr. Caddy, 'and it won't hurt you.'

Mr. Dobbin decided to leave the sea to his betters. He left the next day.

For a time no other fisherman tried to tame the sea or to get a living out of it.

Though the sea couldn't be tamed, the meadows and fields of Mockery Gap were another matter. These fields partook of the customs and traditions of men and women. If you touched the fields they would respond to the touch; and only the most out-of-the-way corners had any kind of native wildness about them.

The lane to the hill, that had once in very olden times been a cliff, always recognised the pretty tread of Mary Gulliver's feet when she walked there leading her horse to grass; and Mr. Caddy's pond at the end of Mr. Caddy's lane knew Mr. Caddy so well that it was near becoming a speaking companion instead of a dumb pond. And Mr. Caddy regarded the ducks and the pond in the light of true and tried friends.

If a realm, settled and solidified, hath the three estates to boast of, so indeed have every small village. The separate conditions of men are not marked upon them alone by their polite speech or tailor-made clothes, for the very lanes they live in and the paths to their homes brand their caste upon them.

No gentleman of the first estate at Mockery could ever have been expected to get a living from the sea, and none except those who belonged to the third would ever go down to it to fish.

The second estate was represented by the village green, the roots of an elm, and a grassy path that led to Mr. Gulliver's small farm-house.

Beside the green was Mrs. Moggs' shop, that had the proper appearance of modest affluence that the green also reflected because it was so near. In the shop and upon the green a decent behaviour that naturally goes with the middle order of being was expected to be seen. And when the first estate stooped to enter this domain it very properly showed by its polite manner of speaking that every civilised village is welded and held together by its middle.

The road that typified the first estate was by the right of long custom called 'The Church Way.' Here there lived the Pinks and the Pattimores, and along a real drive with real gravel there lived Farmer Cheney, who by reason of his money-bags had acquired this place of honour.

The third estate was the children.

These children, though some lived along the Church Way beside the vicarage garden gate, had pulled all who belonged to them, even though their parents might wish to rise, deep down into the mire of the lowest degree. The children pulled with them their teacher Mrs. Topple who suffered from a bad leg and deserved a better one.

The village school was an unlocked prison, for it kept the children in durance for only a short part of the day; and when Mrs. Topple opened the door and let the wretches free, the two upper estates bemoaned the lack of a village constable.

The boundaries of Mockery are important.

In front of Mockery, to the south, was the untamed and variable element, now noisy and now quiet, now high and now low—the sea. To the north was the hill. To the east a country of stone walls, rough stony fields, and

4

a people who were said never to shut the door after them when they went out of a room. To the west there was the Mockery wood, the other side of which, if you walked far enough and didn't mind being a stranger to the cows you met, you might find an aunt to talk to, or even a Squire Roddy if you reached Weyminster.

In every village almost that we can think of, and Mockery was no exception, there is a blind lane that leads nowhere, or at least, if it does lead somewhere, 'tis but to a cottage and a pond, and there the lane ends. No lane could better suggest a good path to somewhere than did Mr. Caddy's. It curved temptingly down a little hill, and at the end of thirty yards there was the pond and nothing more, except Mr. Caddy's cottage, that any one could see from the road, from which road a child could easily have thrown a stone into the pond.

Most of the Mockery cottages belonged, owing to the children living there, to the third estate, and clung together to the Mockery lanes like apples to their parent branch, in an amiable manner that showed friendliness. Two cottages, however, stood at bay and glared at one another, generally with their doors open, like angry dogs. In these two houses, near to the vicarage, lived the Prings and the Pottles, who for more than one generation had hated one another.

All the three estates of the little Mockery world were hardly ever permitted to take a moderate view of one another, because of the children, and because of the quarrel between the Prings and the Pottles; although it must be owned that a certain quieter element was always being introduced by Mr. Caddy, with his tales, rather carnal than otherwise, that he told his ducks, that acted as gentle oil upon the third estate if they happened to hear them. But we should have begun with the highest.

The vicar of Mockery, the Rev. Pattimore, who was just married, though from his sermons one wouldn't have guessed it, was one of those people whose cheek-bones are a little too large and whose frame inclines a little to leanness, and whose mouth, though the lips are full enough, is weak. The appearance of Mr. Pattimore when watched sweeping into little heaps the autumn leaves upon his drive denoted a man ambitious to do right, and ambitious to show the world how rightly he did by becoming some one important. As a rule Mr. Pattimore wore black clothes, but he kept a grey coat to put on when he swept up the leaves. His hair was touched by new silver sixpences, and was fitted to his head a little too closely, for it never, even when his mind was troubled, became ruffled or disturbed. Mr. Pattimore was a very moral man.

Mr. Cheney, the large Mockery farmer,

who possessed money, flocks and herds, and a son named Simon, had a long beard, that he would button into his coat. He owned much, but he wanted more, and had often been noticed, when prying about in his fields, to pick up in his hands anything that looked yellow as if it might be gold.

Mrs. Cheney was a lady with long nails that were generally dirty ones.

No one even in London can control his own destiny, and no one in Mockery Gap ever tried to. In Mockery the most noisy event (if you except the doings of the sea) that could never be altered or soothed down was the quarrel between the Prings and the Pottles. In the simple and ordinary round of Mockery life this quarrel took a chief place, and who could help this—certainly not Mr. Pattimore—when the cottages stared at one another so wrathfully? The tale of this Mockery quarrel went further than the boundaries of the village. For when Mr. Told of Norbury or Mr. Tasker of Shelton happened to mention Mockery, just for something to open the way to a deal in pigs, Mockery would be set down and explained with this remark, ''Tis where folk do quarrel, they Prings and Pottles.'

'But Mr. Pink do live there too,' Mr. Tasker might say to Mr. Told, hoping thereby to prevent the farmer from looking too closely at the pigs he wished to buy. 'So 'e do,'

Mr. Told would reply unthinkingly. And so to the credit of Mockery Mr. Pink did, being a man who had ideas above the common, that were forgiving ones. Mr. Pink had long legs, and a head that wasn't quite as large as it should have been for a man with such feelings.

Mr. Pink lived with his sister, Miss Pink, who had her feelings too, loving feelings, and she once went so far as to write a letter to Mr. Gulliver, a widower and the smaller farmer of Mockery, about them, handing the said letter to Mr. Pring, who was known to be the safest deliverer of a note or message that ever was.

Every one in Mockery, as elsewhere, has a special elevation that can be noted and watched with interest. For no human being can live anywhere without showing some fine attribute— though this may be more imaginary than real —that can bring him to honour. To this, of course, there must ever be an exception—the young girls. They have their natural inclinations, but these inclinations never become fixed in any art or fancy that can separate them from others of their kind. The young girls can be only said to make a number of tales and stories of sufficient variety to be worth the telling to Mr. Caddy's ducks, but none of their arts or actions show that individuality of character that can set a person aside to be pointed out by his neighbours to be a wonder.

It could never have been said about a young Mockery girl, as it was about Mr. Pattimore, that, besides having to his credit the most moral of sermons, he was also supposed to be extremely clever in the art of flying a kite.

One fact of Mockery life we may note here, for it refers to the acts by the doing of which a man is most honoured; and that is, that what a man did was never placed so importantly as what a man was supposed to understand or what he was supposed to be able to do.

No one ever honoured Mr. Caddy the more for his stories, though so much bedroom furniture came into them; but every one knew, and gave Mr. Caddy the right praise for it, that he was the only one in Mockery who understood the ways, the manners, and the customs of the sea.

'Don't 'ee never go down there,' was the wise advice that Mrs. Pring gave to Mr. Dobbin when he first visited the village, 'without thee speak to Mr. Caddy about thik sea.'

And when Mr. Dobbin was leaving the village to go to Maidenbridge, where Mr. James Tarr lived who had once employed him, he couldn't help remarking to Mr. Caddy, whom he met in the road, 'If I had only asked you, Mr. Caddy, how to take a green lobster out of a pot I would never have missed half a finger.'

''Tis its manners,' replied Mr. Caddy,

nodding his head to the sea as if he knew it only too well, 'that bain't particular.'

Mr. Caddy looked at his ducks, that had wandered, as they often used to do, into the road.

''Tain't every one that do understand they waves and fishes,' he said.

Mr. Dobbin looked moodily at Mr. Caddy.

It is not easy to be exactly sure, as every writer should be, how the people of Mockery, who were no book-readers, came to regard Mr. Gulliver as a traveller to far countries and as a viewer of strange fowls and creatures in them. This idea could hardly have arisen in the Mockery mind because Mr. Gulliver's boots were always so old and worn and his hair so dishevelled, as though he had lived for a long time in a country where there were no barbers or cobblers. It is more likely that Mr. Gulliver's reputation as a traveller may have come from a tale of his own experiencing when one market day he had gone to Stone-bridge to buy a new churn. A train had stopped at Tadnol, and Mr. Gulliver had stepped into it supposing that it must also stop at Stonebridge for him to step out again. In the railway carriage there happened to be a reverend gentleman who liked to know about other people, and who looked for some minutes very hard at the farmer as if to read his very soul.

'I believe your name is——?' requested the gentleman. 'Gulliver,' replied the farmer. 'A traveller,' said the gentleman, 'to strange places.'

Mr. Gulliver felt his importance growing very high. He was indeed become a traveller, for the train, an express, had only stopped at Tadnol because the signal was against it, and now ran through Stonebridge.

Besides Gulliver, Mrs. Topple too was praised for what she never had done or never could do. Mrs. Topple was the schoolmistress of Mockery, and every one believed that no one beside her could so well control the ill-doings of a naughty child.

When any child in the village performed some doughty act more than usually atrocious, such as spitting at or kicking his own parent, Mrs. Topple would be sent for. And when she came she would take a cup of tea and complain about her bad leg, and now and again she would look at the child as though it ought never to have been there. She had once remarked into her teacup, 'I fear they leave all their best manners behind in the school.'

Chapter 2

THE BLIND COW

A GROUP of men and women, who all looked as if they had come out for a very important reason, but didn't wish to appear to be doing anything unusual, removed themselves one sunny day in March—each holding an umbrella or an overcoat—from a large and many-seated pleasure car that had stopped upon a grassy down which overlooked both the inland country spaces and the sea waves.

A fox is known by its brush, a lemur by its scream, and a postman by his loud, sharp knock; and our ladies and gentlemen can be known at once, by the extreme care that each bestows upon finding his own stick or umbrella, as the field club of the county.

Once safely out of the car, and grateful for being still in possession of their movable property, the company stood about in threes, and for want of anything better to do they looked at the sea.

Each member of the party looked at the sea as if it had been placed there on purpose to interest them, but was, now that they saw it, a very poor kind of show and hardly worth the journey to view.

There was simply the ordinary blue, with the rocky island beyond, that Mr. James Tarr had so often given them lectures about, that was connected, they knew, to the mainland by a broad and continuous line of heaped and stupid pebbles of a flat shape.

The sea, with its rocky island behind it, had so little to say to one member of the field club—Miss Frances Ogle—that she looked in the other direction towards the land.

There she saw wide spaces, hills in the distance, and woods a little nearer. The wide spaces, as she looked to the right or to the left, became other wide spaces, and the hills became merely other hills. When Miss Ogle tried to look further, she encountered a dimness that might have been anything from a cloud to a church tower, or whatever else the onlooker's fancy might wish it to be.

Miss Ogle now drew her gaze in a little and looked at the wide sweep of the nearer downs that shone green and clear in the midday March sunshine. She noticed some sheep lying down at a distance, and so imbued was she with the learned discoveries in the matter of old transformations made by Mr. Roddy, the president of the club, that for a moment Miss Ogle believed the sheep to be a muster of ancient stones.

The sheep, however, were good enough to express themselves as moderns by rousing and scattering at the loud barking of the shepherd's dog.

Miss Ogle was glad she hadn't spoken, and

turned quickly to the sea and pointed at some
thing—in order to put herself right with the
learned as well as with nature—that, if it wasn't
a whale, must be a stone.

The object that Miss Ogle was pointing at
appeared to be the one thing that pushed itself
out of all the garish prettiness of the spring
day, and was something that was consciously
itself.

This was a black rock.

'Look,' said Miss Ogle, unable to contain
her ideas any longer, 'there's a petrified cow
in the sea; please, Mr. Roddy, do get it up
one day and put it in your museum.'

Miss Ogle had gone a little away from the
others when she made this remark, and those
who heard her speak merely supposed that
she was exclaiming about the beautiful view.
But however wrong Miss Ogle had been about
the sheep, she was right this time, for the rock
that she had pointed to was called 'The Blind
Cow.' For the simple Mockery minds who
lived in the near neighbourhood of the cow
had always supposed, and the story was handed
down from one generation to another, that a
cow which had lost its sight had walked out
upon a hot midsummer day upon the sands,
as cows will do sometimes. But this one
being blind, and thinking that it was merely
crossing a little river to reach green meadows
upon the other side, swam out of its depth

and was drowned. And so the rock came by its name.

But however important to our story Miss Ogle's discovery had been, none of the assembled company noticed it, because each was wondering what kind of learned remark would be first uttered, and whether Mr. James Tarr or Mr. Roddy would be the first to utter it. Meanwhile, and until the learned thing came, the company stood about and gazed at the distant sea a little disparagingly, as though they said, 'If only we had gone on driving in the car, we might have been still listening to conversation that certainly would have been of more interest than the sound of distant waves.' For the car drive upon such an occasion as the present would provide exactly the proper whirl and swing to loose the pretty tongues of scandal, that would wag merrily, although Squire Roddy, the senior member and head of the party, would look sadly at his new gloves and allow five minutes to pass without saying one single word.

During the drive the merry tongues had settled upon two families, the Pinks and the Pattimores, who lived in Mockery village, that was likely to be visited amongst other places where old things might be found.

'I for one wouldn't put up with such treatment,' Miss Ogle had said sternly to Mr. Gollop, who was at the moment deeply wondering whether Miss Ogle's income was really as high as it was said to be, so that if he married her they could afford a pretty servant.

'No,' said Miss Ogle, as the car swayed a little to the side of the road, 'if my husband treated me as Mr. Pattimore does his wife—I should leave him.'

'But it's Mr. Pattimore's open opinion,' said Mr. Roddy harmlessly, 'and one that is founded upon the Scriptures, that married people should live as though they were not married.'

'But she's so nice,' said Miss Ogle, looking at Mr. Gollop, 'and he's not fit to be a clergyman.'

'Why not?' inquired Mr. James Tarr, who always liked to put people to rights; 'for I do not understand why a man who happens to believe in chastity shouldn't be a clergyman.'

'But the clergy have such clever families,' said Miss Ogle.

Mr. James Tarr stared hard at a church they were passing. 'They can't help that,' he said.

'I have been told,' said Miss Ogle, for the motion of the car always kept her talking, 'that Mr. Pattimore sleeps far away from her in an attic——'

Mr. Roddy looked up from his gloves.

'Mr. Pink, you know is my agent, and he lives near to the sea, and that's where we're going,' he said quietly.

'Oh yes, I've heard about him,' Miss Ogle replied, laughing.

Mr. Roddy held out his gloved hand and touched a tree that the car swayed nearly into as it passed a cart in the road. It was always like that during the drive: there were things that could be said, but when once the goal was reached and the green grass trod upon, or the castle stones, and the real business of the day commenced, the very simplest conversation was always out of reach and scandal was silenced.

And now that the drive was over, even Miss Ogle felt the same difficulty as all the other members of the party about what should be said or done.

But Miss Ogle was a resourceful lady, and so she dropped her walking-stick. Mr. Roddy picked it up, and Miss Ogle, in an offhand manner that no one but she would have dared to use upon such an important occasion, invited Mr. Roddy to climb a large tumulus that happened to be there, and to tell them how rocks were made.

Although this setting of Mr. Roddy up above all the others was quite unseemly and utterly out of the order of the day at that point in the proceedings, yet Mr. Roddy climbed the mound, abstracting from his pocket as he did so a parcel of typed notes relating to the life-history of cliffs, valleys, hills, and rivers.

Even extremely gifted people, who wear really expensive stockings, at least the gentlemen, and the ladies with their fine walking-shoes, must look at something besides gorse bushes and rabbit-holes. And our fine ones, each surrounded with a cloak of the grand manners, having eyes, watched. And what they saw was—and they all blamed Miss Ogle for bringing about a scene so discreditable to the common decencies practised by field societies— that Mr. James Tarr had begun to climb the tumulus at the same moment as Mr. Roddy, only from the other side. Mr. James Tarr was a gentleman of an argumentative temper, whose favourite remark was, 'I wish to do it my own way.' And his own way in this case was to spring in leaps up the mound, and to encounter, with his rugged and determined countenance looking more grim than usual, mild Mr. Roddy at the top of it.

'You can't both talk at once, you know,' Miss Ogle most shamefully called out, 'though you may want to.'

Every one looked anywhere but at Miss Ogle.

'Don't you two begin to fight up there,' she called louder than ever.

It was most fortunate that Mr. Gollop was of the party.

'Come,' he said, leading Miss Ogle gently but firmly away by the arm, 'do look at those birds in the bushes.'

Every one now was relieved, and also most grateful to the Rev. Alfred Gollop for having saved their ears, at least at the moment, from any more of Miss Ogle.

'Those birds aren't larks,' said Mr. Gollop, letting go the lady's arm and going nearer to the gorse bushes so that he could see the birds more distinctly.

'What are they, then?' inquired the lady.

'I think they're sparrows,' said Mr Gollop innocently, but the lady had turned to the mound again.

And there Mr. Roddy—for Mr. James Tarr had descended again—was explaining in a mild and almost an apologetic voice, very different from His that made it, what the seemingly stupid affairs of nature were really all about.

Pointing with his glove, he was saying when Miss Ogle returned from watching the sparrows, 'To the westward, by Weyminster Bay, there the oolites live, which form a cushion; below these are potter's and pile clay, firebricks, bituminous shales, sheep and cattle, potatoes and cider, and for the meadows the catch-water plan is used.'

'And what kind of plan is that?' asked Miss Ogle simply.

Mr. Roddy shook his head and came down; he saw the vital necessity, if Miss Ogle continued to come to their meetings, of impressing her with the real seriousness of these occasions.

The most simple way to do this appeared to Mr. Roddy to be to make himself look grand in her eyes.

In order to do so in the way that he thought to be most telling, Mr. Roddy picked up from the grass a handful of little white shells.

These little shells he showed to Miss Ogle. 'They are called by my name,' he said; 'they are Roddites, and I am the discoverer of them.'

Miss Ogle looked at the shells carelessly. 'Pretty Roddites,' she said, and then without a word to the discoverer of them she called out, 'And now I've seen the Roddites I want Mr. James Tarr to tell me about that little church in the valley.'

Mr. Tarr sprang to the top of the mound again in three leaps.

'Mockery Church,' he said, taking out some notes, though written ones, as Mr. Roddy had done, and pointing down into the valley with them, 'is a cruciform edifice of stone; it possesses an embattled tower that contains only one bell, while the church itself affords one hundred and eighty-two sittings.

'The word Mockery is derived, of course, from Monksbury, and that word explains itself.'

'It doesn't explain itself to me.' interrupted Miss Ogle, who was the only listener who had really listened to Mr. Tarr.

Mr. Tarr stepped down; to be interrupted

at all was more than he could usually bear, but to be interrupted by a lady who had only joined the club a week before, and didn't belong to any county family, was no petty rudeness but a high aggravation.

And now something occurred that went near to breaking up the party, out of sheer horror at the incident; for Miss Ogle mounted the tumulus in the place of Mr. Tarr, and said, excitingly waving her walking-stick, that she wanted to speak too.

When he saw that she really meant to address them, Mr. Roddy began collecting the Roddites again, and making a little heap of them that he intended to carry home with him later; while Mr. James Tarr, whose temper was of another colour, said boldly to those near to him that 'he would throw Miss Ogle into the sea, if the sea had only the decency to flow up to the tumulus as it once did one hundred million years ago.'

When Miss Ogle had reached a point in her discourse and was talking about the edible octopus, a fish that a poor fisherman of Mockery, Mr. Dobbin, had once offered her—when trying to sell his catch in the town—for a shilling, she happened to look below her and saw that the hill was deserted.

Chapter 3

THE NELLIE-BIRD

THE Assyrian, when he came down 'like a wolf,' so the poet says, could never have shown such a spying audacity as our learned society when it strayed about, each member going his or her own way, in the little village called Mockery Gap.

They found the country people, as Miss Ogle said during the drive home, 'so nice to talk to, and so ready,' the lady added, 'to show you the way to the church.'

Having never been visited before so wholeheartedly by the learned, the people of Mockery had lived for generations most patiently, and, when the passions from on high or from below allowed them time, both mildly and contentedly. But now, alas! all—at least for a few months—would be different, the old order giving place to new error, and merely because it wasn't in Mr. James Tarr's habit of life to leave well alone.

Mr. James Tarr was the last gentleman in the world, with the exception perhaps of one other, to allow any earthly paradise, where wild roses scent the air in June, to remain without ambitions as every real paradise should.

Mr. Tarr liked to be remembered as one who carried with him, and handed it free and gratis to those he met, a fine zeal in the matter

22

of discoveries. And not discoveries alone, for Mr. Tarr, when he sniffed the air of a new village, would delight to darkly insinuate that something might be going to happen, or else some one might be going to come, that would throw into the shade all events heretofore, and prepare the place for new happenings of terror or excitement. Besides general prognostication, Mr. Tarr would set the minds of simple people running in other ways, too, than by foretelling momentous things. He believed that he alone in all the world really knew what to recommend to give another person a proper incitement to live, which was, as Mr. Tarr would be sure to point out, to hunt for something that was almost, if not entirely, impossible to be found.

Mr. Tarr was, amongst all men, the one who knew, and the one who could start in the mind of the most harmless hedge-priest maybe the rather foolish idea that the poor man might one day become a person of importance.

'If you spend your whole life,' Mr. Tarr would say impressively, 'in looking for a centipede with only ninety-nine legs, you will be happy.'

He had given a young portrait-painter whom he had once met in an Essex marsh this advice, who took it literally, and spent the rest of his life upon his knees in damp rushes and low deserted hollows.

When the company quitted the mound upon which was Miss Ogle, Mr. James Tarr, with his head thrust a little forward, looked down upon Mockery, and settled determinedly that it was a place that must be excited into action.

A man at work in a field, near to the smaller of the two village farms, caught his attention. Mr. Tarr looked at the motions of this man, who was spreading manure in a slow and thoughtful manner, and he thought he knew him.

'That's Gulliver,' said Mr. Tarr, going down the hill in the man's direction, 'and those heaps are dung and not mole-hills; and I've got a present for him.'

Mr. Tarr lived at Maidenbridge, where Mr. Gulliver, the small farmer of Mockery, would drive sometimes to sell his butter, and Mr. Tarr had noticed the earnest manner and the gentle care with which the smallholder handled his goods at the doors of his customers' houses.

Mr. Tarr didn't spend much time in talking to Mr. Gulliver, because he meant to set on fire with new ideas other minds too, so he merely handed to Mr. Gulliver an envelope that contained, he said, a map of the world for him to look at in the evenings.

'Your name is Gulliver, you know,' said Mr. Tarr impressively, as he turned away and strode jauntily in the direction of the village school.

With such visitors about, so that the excitement in Mockery Gap had grown intense, the school-children, whose general endeavours went the natural way of much noise and shouting, were for a moment or two stilled, and especially those who stood near to Mr. James Tarr when he talked to the schoolmistress, Mrs. Topple.

Mr. James Tarr had walked at the school wall as if he intended to walk through it, but stopped suddenly just as he was going to strike his head, and eyed a stone that had jutted out a little, and informed Mrs. Topple that the stone was a Saxon one.

Mrs. Topple was a lady, pale and sad looking, and no wonder with those children about; and she supposed that every gentleman who wasn't Mr. Hunt the town postmaster, or Mr. Best the school inspector, was a doctor. And so, as soon as Mr. Tarr had finished telling her about the stone she told him about her bad leg. Mr. Tarr looked over the heads of the listening children, who were quieted for the moment, into the green fields of Mockery, as though seeking inspiration. He wished to give to Mrs. Topple a lasting remembrance of himself, and so he said, with the certainty that his character was famed for, 'Surely, madam, if you searched in all those green fields, that I am told go all the way down to the sea, you might find a stalk of clover with four leaves.'

Mrs. Topple's face brightened. Here was a fine doctor indeed!

'All your woes will go then, when you once find that clover,' said Mr. Tarr.

It was then, after setting a light to Mrs. Topple, that Mr. Tarr turned upon the children and told them about the Nellie-bird.

'Voyagers mention,' he began, in the same buoyant tone in which he addressed the society, 'according to Stanley's history of birds, a species of albatross called the Nellie-bird, *Diomedea spadicea*. One day or one night that bird will come to Mockery; watch for it.' And Mr. Tarr strode off.

There was a portion of an old building that is sometimes found that always, more than any other part or portion, interested Mr. Tarr, and this was a buttress.

He was examining one of these that helped to hold up the old wall of the great Mockery barn, when he was aware that his investigation —he was pushing the buttress in a friendly way to see how firm it was—was being closely regarded by the eyes of Mr. Cheney, the largest Mockery farmer.

Mr. Cheney, who evidently fancied that the gentlemanly visitor was really intending to overturn the buttress, remarked feelingly: ''Tain't likely, do 'ee think, that there be any golden coins hidden under they wold brick leanings, for 'tis only silver that me poor boy Simon do 'ave for 'is spending wi' they maidens.'

Mr. Tarr looked triumphantly at the farmer —here was a fine soil indeed in which to plant the exciting seeds of ambition. He motioned to Mr. Cheney to step back a pace or two; from whence the tumulus, that was left solitary and at the mercy of only Miss Ogle, who was still standing there, could be plainly seen.

Mr. Tarr pointed to the mound.

'Under the mound,' he said, 'where you see that woman'—Miss Ogle descended as though she had heard herself mentioned so rudely— 'all the golden earrings that the concubines of the ancient Britons would wear so grandly are hidden; you have only to dig there deeply enough to find—gold.'

Leaving the farmer standing and still looking inquiringly up at the mound, Mr. James Tarr strode happily along the Mockery lanes. He wasn't the moon, and yet he had started tides flowing; he wasn't the king, and yet he had put thoughts and ambitions into virgin hearts. He was still desirous, and he looked. He looked into the tiny Mockery shop that was also the post-office, and entered to buy a stamp and to entice out of Widow Moggs the shopkeeper all her hopes and feelings. Mrs. Moggs, who had already been visited by nearly every one in the party, stood nervously behind her counter and shook her bells, the two curls that hung on either side of her head.

'You are lonely here, Mrs. Moggs,' said Mr. Tarr to her, having noticed her name upon the door, 'and you want a pair of white mice to keep you happy.'

Mrs. Moggs rung her bells. She rather liked Mr. Tarr; he was evidently quite another person from the ill-mannered postmaster who sometimes came from Maidenbridge in his motor.

'Mr. Pink says,' replied Mrs. Moggs timidly, 'that I ought to go one summer's day and look at the beautiful sea.'

'Perhaps you should,' said Mr. Tarr, taking up the stamp that he had bought but forgotten to pay for; 'but you will never really be happy without those white mice.'

As soon as any village or tract of the country-side had yielded up all its ancient history, culled from the gravestones, its grassy terraces, and its silent valleys, to the prying eyes and hammer-taps of the grand and learned, then would these fine hunters, with one accord, as eagles to the carcass, crowd into the vicarage dining-room for tea.

Here they would be welcomed by the lady of the house and by the gentleman, both wishing to give them all the honour that they could, and currant cake.

And here to the Mockery vicarage came Mr.

James Tarr, who read plainly enough—being taller than the others—the writing, or rather the painting, upon the wall of the dining-room.

This painting was the portrait of a Dean who was believed to be, and truthfully so, Mr. Pattimore's relation.

'That's what he wishes to be,' said Mr. Tarr to himself, allowing Mr. Pattimore's whole past and future to remain agape for preferment, and for ever to be so.

Passing him by as so settled, Mr. Tarr did just notice Mrs. Pattimore, a very child in her looks and blushes, whose lips, red as cherries, asked for better things than to reply to Miss Ogle's questions about chair-covers.

'Mr. and Miss Pink, this is Mr. Tarr,' exclaimed Mr. Roddy, seeing Mr. Tarr desire to catch those two simple ones in a corner.

Mr. James Tarr being thus introduced, sat in front of his meek prey as if to prevent the least chance of their escape, and said, looking sternly at Mr. Pink, who was if anything the meeker of the two, 'Something will happen here, I feel sure, Mr. Pink.'

No one had taken the trouble to hand to Mr. Pink the least portion of currant cake, and so now with hunger in his heart he turned to his sister, hoping that she would answer this gentleman from the town, who looked a fierce one.

Mr. Tarr turned too to Miss Pink. 'There is something about Mockery Gap,' he said, speaking loudly, so as to be heard above the clatter of tongues and tea-cups, 'that is very dreadful and ominous. I am certain that one day something will happen here. I shouldn't be surprised if one dreadful day something might be seen.'

Miss Pink couldn't shut her eyes, so she looked down; she saw a flower in the carpet that took the shape in her mind of a horrid beast with horns and a tail.

'It's that beast,' she thought, 'that will come—the dreadful beast from the book of Revelation.'

Miss Pink had all her life been afraid of crawling things; she had always expected to meet a spider one day in Mockery with a head like Farmer Cheney's bull, and now here was the very horror being expected by a rich and angry gentleman from Maidenbridge.

'Will it come from the sea?' she asked, looking up timidly at Mr. Tarr.

Mr. Tarr nodded impressively.

'Oh,' sighed Miss Pink, 'how dreadful!'

Mr. Tarr looked at Mr. Pink, and decided that he would be happy as a Methodist preacher.

'The country people are ignorant here,' he remarked forcefully; 'they are low in the scale of being; they are like underdone mutton, they want to be baked by salvation, they're all bloody.'

'I fear they're not always as kind to one another as they should be,' said Mr. Pink; 'and as I am Mr. Roddy's representative, I am forced to hear a great deal that I am sorry for.'

'The people want salvation,' said Mr. Tarr.

'They want kindness,' said Mr. Pink.

Mr. Pink leaned forward, so that his simple, placid face, long and sallow, and hung with a yellow moustache like a faded and dusty curtain, almost touched Mr. Tarr's ruggedness. A look of wistful hope came to him, and he said, looking first to see that Mr. Pattimore was as far away as the length of the vicarage dining-room allowed him to be, 'Yes, yes, you are right: they want to be saved from those children, Mr. Tarr.'

'That are such a trouble to poor Mrs. Moggs,' sighed Miss Pink, 'and to Mrs. Topple.'

A silence now came to the vicarage dining-room that left only Miss Ogle speaking.

'I have learnt so much to-day,' said Miss Ogle, 'that I feel quite another person.'

Mr. Gollop looked at the servant, who was a pretty one; he also peered about amongst the crumbs under the table—he had lost his handkerchief.

Miss Ogle found it for him.

'We had better be going now, I think,' said Mr. Roddy, shaking hands with Mr. Pattimore and looking up at the Dean; 'because we have the hill to climb, you know.'

'And the Roddites to collect,' whispered Miss Ogle, and laughed sillily.

Vaguely, and with no enthusiasm now, for a coldness had crept into their hearts from the sea perhaps, the company, with the exception of Mr. Tarr, who met Mr. Gulliver in the lane and had a last word with him about his travels, climbed the hill and settled themselves in the car again.

'Mr. Tarr's always the latest to come,' said Mr. Roddy, when that gentleman at last seated himself beside the driver.

'That's because he's so clever,' whispered Miss Ogle to Mr. Gollop.

The car started, and the blind cow out at sea saw the hill bare again.

Chapter 4

A WARNING

THE hill, or Mockery cliff as it was usually called by those who lived near, might have smiled, could a hill smile, at the fine visitors who had peopled it and then departed, leaving only their wheel-marks, and a scented handkerchief dropped by Miss Ogle, behind them.

Mockery lay below, and showed from this point of vantage, if carefully looked down upon —for one often misses a building or two when the land and the cottages grow into one another—a farmhouse, a smaller one, a white lane and a green, fields that almost touch the sea, and here and there the glitter of a tiny stream, and also a pleasant wood. The vicarage and church had settled meekly in the folds of the valley as hardly to be noticed, and even when seen they only appeared to point to Mr. Pink's stone house that stood by the church lane, and to say that 'it shouldn't have been there.'

Mockery cliff must have found the noise of the waves tiresome in past years, and so moved itself complacently backwards little by little, allowing the pretty meadows to be formed, proud of their cowslips; and the lanes and houses; and of course man.

In its backward proceeding the cliff had risen to a fine height, so that John Wesley, who found the people hereabouts as gentle as lambs, called it a mountain. It may have been—in this matter of moving mountains—the faith of Mr. Gulliver's great-grandfather, who always said that the small-holding of the family should be larger, which it now was.

For if it is easy by faith to cast a mountain into the sea, it should be just as easy, and better for the sheep—and the movement wasn't expected to happen in one second of human time, but rather in one of God's moments—to get the mountain, or any mountain, out of the sea and to push it by faith inland.

The mere daytime of prettiness departed with the town visitors, and now that they were gone the true look of the land, that had been hidden from them, came forth again to be seen by those who have eyes to see. The blind-cow rock, that alone of all natural objects had never been beguiled by the sunbeams into looking pretty, now took upon it as the sun declined, giving the true bass note to the colours of the evening, the blackness of despair. The blind cow now began to spread out her influence further than herself, the waves that struck the rock became intense and living. Its dead state, as the abodes of the dead will sometimes do, reached out hands to form, to grave, and to portray, and to cast over Mockery the feelings and the fears of the night.

Clouds that earlier in the day had been but shining vapour, now became real and yet more real and grew sensibly darker. The cliff, the fields below, the church that waited for the night, even the tiny shining of the little water-brooks, were beginning to express the supreme loveliness of lonely silence—of the beauty that dies.

Shadows, born of the shadow of the blind cow, began to creep here and there like monstrous toads and thick vipers. The shadows became more and more monstrous as the sun dropped, while some amongst them now showed a likeness to him that is called Man, a dweller upon the earth.

And now the sea, more than any other emanation of eternal truth, changed its face. The sea darkened, the dainty spaces above the waters where the light was began to take up the shadows of the deep and to wear them as a garment, while the tumulus upon the cliff watched as if glad that the evening was come.

This green mound, about which the spirit of an ancient and buried king still hovered, was the same from whence, when the company were departed, Miss Ogle had addressed the seagulls. It was also the grave within which, as Mr. Tarr had informed the Mockery farmer, golden earrings were buried.

Ever since the people of Mockery had raised the mound over the bones of their king, who had died about the time of the great flood, the king's spirit had brooded there, and had watched the inhabitants of the village of Mockery.

He liked Mr. Caddy, who hadn't for some years now taken the trouble to work for a living, for Mrs. Caddy did the work while Mr. Caddy told the stories; all of which contained night-time or, as Mr. Caddy would have said, bedtime matters.

And Mr. Caddy wouldn't always confine himself to such simple subjects, for he would sometimes—and the heathen ghost liked to hear him—mention his betters.

'They do say,' Mr. Caddy had been heard to remark, 'that wold God be everywhere—but 'E bain't where I be, and that I do know. Parson do a-preach of, an' even Mr. Pink 'ave a-named 'E; and some do tell that 'twere God who made the wide roaring sea, and the more fool 'E to make en, so I do say. But I do believe,' and here Mr. Caddy would wink slyly, 'that 'E did a-make each pretty maiden.'

Even though the one who rested in the mound for ever liked Mr. Caddy, he had no love for Mr. James Tarr, and so he decided, did Farmer Cheney come to dig there, he would be greeted with some accident or trouble or ever he found the golden earrings.

Chapter 5

'DON'T STRAY'

APPARENTLY Mr. James Tarr paid no heed to the young women that he met when about his grandmother's business; for old Mrs. Tarr had always said that people should have an interest in life.

Had he done so, he could hardly have failed to notice Mary Gulliver, who was gathering sticks in the hedge when he gave her father the map he had promised him some days before. Mary had noticed Mr. Tarr and had wished he had spoken to her, because men were the kind of creatures that Mary liked far better than cows or sheep if they came near to her.

When Mary was very young, and her blushes were so many that they were become her true complexion, she had permitted Simon Cheney, the young man who was most sought after by the Mockery girls, to take her up to the green mound.

Simon did so, as Mary wished, who felt as he kissed her that she really was a girl in petticoats.

Soon after young Simon had first kissed Mary, her mother had, for no reason unless she was grown tired of making butter, walked one May morning into the sea. Some said that she did so because Mr. Tarr, in whose service she had been before she was married, advised her more than once to be very careful to keep her husband at home because of his name. 'Mrs. Gulliver feared to lose him, and so she went first,' was how Miss Pink saw the matter.

As soon as Mrs. Gulliver's body was laid under the corner elm in the Mockery church-yard, to the great entertainment of the pack of Mockery children who had watched the pro-ceedings, the Rev. John Pattimore returned with the bereaved family to their cottage, and, sitting in a straight-backed chair with a look that plainly showed he had come there to give a serious warning, he explained to Mr. Gulliver and to Mary all the subtle ways by which a young girl could be led into sin. Mary stared hard at him as if he were addressing her and her father in the Greek tongue, while Mr. Gulliver listened with an eager interest, as though in each corner of the room he was aware that a door to hell was being opened.

'Now that your wife is gone,' said Mr. Pattimore, 'you must guard your daughter with the greatest care; you must prevent her from wandering for too long a time near to the sea; and beware of all nakedness.'

'You don't think, do you,' asked Mr. Gulliver with a scared look, 'that anything might come up to she naked out of they waters?'

'I hope not,' replied Mr. Pattimore, 'but it's best to be careful.'

'And you must never allow her on Sundays to wander in the dark lanes after the evening service, for the lion roars in them . . .'

Mr. Gulliver was an easy-tempered and lovable countryman, who believed everything; and now, after being told that something might come up out of the sea at any moment, or else a lion might roar in the lane, he looked at Mary as though she were the magnet that could draw out of holes in the earth and the deep places in the sea horrid naked monsters.

Mary, whose mind was as simple as her father's, when she heard that, wished to find Simon Cheney and to tell him about the lion; or else, if he wasn't ready to go to the hill with her, she might first find Rebecca Pring or Dinah Pottle and tell them. 'It's a nice and a dreadful thing,' thought Mary, 'that there are beasts that go about in the earth and sea that can hurt a girl.'

Mr. Pattimore held up his hand and looked at Mary. 'Remember,' he said, 'don't stray.'

Mr. Gulliver's farmhouse, the lesser one in Mockery village, was but a cottage drooping and crestfallen, next to which was a stable that the farmer's old horses found suited to their winter need, and a cow stall that pleased the cows in a like manner. These abodes of wood and mud built so long ago and still remaining as a shelter to man and to cattle most surely proved that it's the spirit of man that holds up the house, and that all home-made things last the longest when left to themselves. Whenever one walks in any new place, entering perhaps with Mr. James Tarr and his friends, it is proper to greet each wayside post, each Mrs. Pottle and Mrs. Pring, each Dean and attic bed, as we come to them, in exact sequence. For events fierce or simple should lead us, rather than we them; for if we wish to know what our neighbours are doing, their little dogs, or the sound of their carpets being beaten, can tell us, if we are but willing to wait a moment or two, all the news.

Sometimes a village—and this, a week after the visit of the field club, appeared to be true about Mockery—entirely hides its inhabitants. The rude children who usually rushed the lanes in pursuit of all naughtiness were hidden in school, and the March sun, a fine, splendid thing in its early glory, noticed only that Mary Gulliver was abroad.

Mary indeed felt herself, as she always did, as prettily clothed; but as no one looked upon her as she came out of her door and gazed inquisitively about, she felt in that sudden solitude—for even Mrs. Pring wasn't beside her gate—a sense of the danger that Mr. Pattimore predicted would lie in wait for her after her mother died.

'Something be about,' thought Mary, 'and that I do know.'

She stood uncertainly upon the green, hoping to see a friendly figure or two moving or loitering, but no one was there.

Mary hesitated; should she go and wake her father, who was asleep in his chair after his morning ploughing, and tell him that 'there must be something else about if there wasn't no people'?

The mysterious presence of some hidden danger, that the intuitive feeling of a girl recognises 'as being about,' has a way of adding excitedly to her interest in herself—an interest that can only come by means of fear.

Mary Gulliver's interest in herself—she felt it first in her toes until it crept all over her body —began, not as one would have thought with young Simon Cheney's discoveries, but with the visit of Mr. Pattimore after her mother's funeral. Mary began to think then of herself as something, a collection of all sorts of wishes and hopes, that shouldn't be looked at all over. And so, when she went to bed at night or rose in the morning out of the heavy sleep that her bedroom gave her with its tightly-closed windows, she would cleverly manage that one garment at least always covered her. When Mary washed she did it by halves, for it was always the whole of her, and not as Lear in the play saw the matter, naming one half of a woman as the devil's, that she feared. Mary's look at the world, as the look at herself would have been had the garment fallen, was one of utter astonishment and fear at its nakedness when unclothed. And to Mary the world's best and only clothing was—humankind.

Mary's 'Oh' that she gave now because she saw all Mockery as naked about her, was her usual exclamation with which she met anything that astonished her.

To-day, as there was no skirt or coat to cover the earth, Mary walked a little nervously to the pasture beside the sea where the cows were.

The sea, and especially when she could espy no ship or boat sailing upon it, appeared in her eyes as something very improper in its nakedness.

The land had its trees and gateposts and beasts too, that gave it a sort of covering even though no man or woman was about. But the sea with its wide masculine spaces and the wicked dancing of its waves always made modest Mary blush when she looked upon it, and fancy that one day a naked man, rather than Miss Pink's beast, would come out of it.

Near to the field where Mr. Gulliver's cows were feeding was a deserted fisherman's hut, the last residence of poor Mr. Dobbin who wasn't lucky enough to earn a living by fishing. The hut still had a chimney, and Mary, who didn't like to look at the sea because of its mannish ways as explained by Mr. Caddy, gazed at the hut chimney when she walked across to the corner of the field where the cows were. When she was quite near to the hut Mary was startled to see a puff of white smoke come from the chimney. Mary stood still and trembled. Her simple mind was reasoning with itself: 'There couldn't be smoke,' she decided, 'without fire,' and 'there couldn't be fire unless some one collected sticks and set a light to them.'

'Oh,' gasped Mary, 'I be sure that some one be about,' and she began to drive the cows home.

As Mary milked she couldn't help hoping that Simon Cheney would meet her upon the hill when she led Dick there: Dick being Mr. Gulliver's oldest horse, who wasn't always needed at home, and who was granted the privilege of spending the greater number of his days in calm contentment upon the inland cliff.

Mr. Gulliver, who had been studying for more than one evening now the queer picture, or map rather, that Mr. Tarr had given him, said to Mary as he opened the barton gate for her and the horse:

'Do 'ee mind and run home if anything do meet 'ee in lanes.'

'Children,' said Mary, 'do speak of a Nellie-bird, a nasty naked thing that gentleman 'ave told of.'

Mr. Gulliver looked very grave.

'And there be,' said Mary, who loved to drink up fear till she gasped, 'Miss Pink's wicked beast wi' 'is horns an' tail.'

'And that bain't all,' said Mr. Gulliver, 'for there be elephants and apes in India.'

'Oh, I do hope Simon will meet I,' said Mary. Her father nodded and hoped so too.

Mary was glad, for now the nasty nakedness of the land that had troubled her so when she went out for the cows was covered, for Mr. Caddy, the favourite of the buried king of Mockery, stood by his cottage gate that was a new one. Mr. Caddy was leaning against the gatepost and was watching with a friendly eye his ducks in the pond. Mr. Caddy walked a few steps and came to Mary.

'She do tell I,' he said, referring to his wife and speaking of the ducks, 'that they ducks be a-working while wold Caddy don't do nothing—but ducks do all know that I do lean and talk.'

Mr. Caddy used to lean, having evidently entered into a covenant with his garden gate to hold him up for ever. He talked, too; for no lady, not even Mrs. Pattimore or mild and plain Miss Pink, could pass Mr. Caddy without exchanging a word or two.

The horse, as was natural, stopped beside Mr. Caddy, and Mary stopped too. It was fortunate that she did so at that moment, for

the Mockery children scampered by, led by
Esther, a love-child planted by the war and now
given house-room by her aunt, Mrs. Pottle.

''Tis said,' said Mr. Caddy to Mary when
the noise was gone by, 'that they be children;
an' that all thik noise be a-called up by bedtime
doings.'

'Oh,' said Mary, 'oh, Mr. Caddy, you do
talk about things that you shouldn't.'

Mr. Caddy nodded; he was pleased with
such praise. He now watched with a knowing
and interested look Mary's horse feeding upon
the rich spring clover that grew beside the way.

'You bain't never been down to the sea,
'ave 'ee?' asked Mr. Caddy, who wished to
retain Mary a little longer because he liked her.

'No,' replied Mary, 'an' I shouldn't like to,
for I don't fancy they nasty waves that do rise
up and fall upon any one.'

'True, they bain't proper, they waves bain't,
for a poor maiden to see,' said Mr. Caddy, who
entirely agreed with Mary's attitude towards
rude nature; 'an' they bain't covered by no
other blanket than darkness at night-time,
them waves that do so swell and break.'

Mary looked inquiringly at Mr. Caddy, for
he was always the one to give information
about the sea to any one.

'Do thik sea,' asked Mary, 'that do bide
there beyond fisherman's hut, where chimney
do smoke of itself, go on a-swelling for ever,

or do 'e but cover the bottom sky, same as
clouds do sometimes hide what be up above?'

'No, no, bain't always there,' replied Mr.
Caddy with conviction; 'seas do run off sometimes when they be minded; they do run down
roads far off, shouting out, "The Nellie-bird be
a-coming," same as children do shout—'tis a
strong, happy boy, thik sea be, that do rise
and watch for a maiden.'

Mr. Caddy chanced at this moment to look
up at the green mound upon the cliff; he saw
a figure standing there who wasn't the ancient
king.

Mary laughed; she began to lead the horse
along the lane that led to the cliff. As she
went along she heard Mr. Caddy talking, for
want of any better company, to his ducks; he
was advising them in many wise terms never to
go down to the sea. The ducks had come out
of the ditch and were looking up at Mr. Caddy,
quacking with excitement as if they quite
understood what he was saying and were wide
awake to it.

Mr. Caddy having been seen, had in a kind
of way clothed the earth for Mary, and now
there was Simon Cheney upon the hill, who
would be sure to help to hide the nakedness that nature so improperly exposed. But
she had to get to Simon, and Mary looked
timidly up at the sky as she walked along the
lane leading the horse.

The evening light shone, wonderful in its clearness; there was no cloud. The clear colours burned and cut with the sharp sword of beauty.

Mary couldn't help looking up, because the sky was a great deal too much like the sea in her idea, and she feared that she might behold something in it that she didn't wish to see.

Mary sighed; she looked from the sky to the clear dark line of the Mockery cliff. She shuddered, all was so naked. The cliff, she felt, should be wearing a coat, while the bare sky should at least have the decency to clothe itself in a chemise with pink ribbons.

The elm trees by the lane Mary looked at too a little doubtfully; she hoped they would soon have their summer garments again. She always felt a little nervous going under those bare boughs in the winter time, and now that the spring was come she was glad to see the beginnings of proper clothing.

Every wanderer's walk, whether for business or for pleasure, is an adventure in Mockery; for who can tell what is going to happen or who one will see when the home gate is closed behind and we are out and moving in the lanes? There may be a little white pig running that's escaped from a neighbour's sty; or a waggon of loaded corn part overturned, with the corn sacks lying huge and heavy in the mud of the road; or else an old boot or a child's ribbon—

for one never knows what one's luck will be here upon earth.

And so with Mary; for when she happened to stare into the thick hedge thinking that a rabbit was there, Mrs. Pottle, whose bony body and thin crabbed face expressed anger, crawled out from the ditch, wherein Mary supposed, having so recently been talking to Mr. Caddy, that Mrs. Pottle had been making her bed.

But though Mary was surprised, Dick the horse was more so, and in the excitement of his feeling at seeing Mrs. Pottle so suddenly he broke from Mary and trotted merrily up the lane in the direction of his well-known field.

Mrs. Pottle was not alone, but what at first Mary supposed to be a man was in reality a large knotted lump of wood. And with this awkward-shaped piece of wood, that had she been naked very much resembled the lady's own trunk, Mrs. Pottle began to beat the ground, explaining that the part of the lane that she struck was 'Sarah Pring.'

'She be always hurting I,' shouted Mrs. Pottle, and with every stroke she beat the road harder. When she grew a little tired with the giving of so many blows she threw the wood down and looked at Mary, who had very naturally stepped back a step or two.

'Sarah Pring do say,' said Mrs. Pottle in a mysterious whisper, going nearer to Mary, 'that our Esther bain't got no clothes, only on top.' Mary looked up at the hill; the hill line was as naked as ever, and Mary thought that it ought to have an apron, even though a dirty one like Mrs. Pottle's.

Mary spoke soothingly to Mrs. Pottle; she wished to calm her.

'Little Esther be a good maid, and that I do know,' she said feelingly; 'and whatever badness she do give herself to, 'tain't no naked badness.'

'Yes,' said Mrs. Pottle, somewhat quieted by Mary's praise of her niece, 'I do dress she nice though the poor maid be born so wicked; but thik Caddy do say that all green fields be beds and bedding in war time.'

Mary followed the horse, that was now feeding a little way ahead of her; she was so shocked at Mrs. Pottle's tale of how the white virtue of Esther had been muddied by Mrs. Pring's scandalous words, that she walked slowly instead of hurrying up the hill to the mound where Simon was waiting for her.

Mary was well aware that nothing could sting sharper than country venom when it suggested nakedness. Had any one said about her clothes what was hinted at about Esther's, Mary would have spent many nights in bitter tears.

As it was, she dared not lift up her eyes for some moments, because she feared that the unclothed sky might take upon it the form and semblance of Esther's legs as Mrs. Pring represented them to be. When she did look up it was to behold Miss Pink, standing a little way from the horse, and looking at it as if it were the huge beast come up out of the sea that she so feared.

Mary stood beside the horse and allowed Miss Pink to go by.

Miss Pink, the most demure and harmless little lady in the world, with the grey shawl that she always wore round her shoulders in winter or in summer, and with shoes that went as near to being pattens as any shoe could, stood for a moment when she was gone safely by the horse and looked timidly back at Mary.

Miss Pink's nose was the smallest of its kind ever invented; but however small her nose was, it could always show signs of fear as well as her eyes. It showed real terror now when Miss Pink said, 'Oh, Mary Gulliver, when I first saw the horse I thought it had the face of a lion.' Miss Pink's tiny nose tried to hide in the folds of her shawl.

'You haven't seen anything to-day, have you,' she asked even more timorously, 'coming up out of the sea?'

'Yes, there be something about,' replied Mary, 'for fisherman's chimney do smoke where there bain't no one.'

Miss Pink looked towards the sea. A column of white smoke rose up into the still evening air from the deserted cottage.

Chapter 6

GOD SIMON

OFTEN in the country a young farmer's son, whose parents are rich, is so fattened and reddened by praise and good living that he becomes a sort of man-god, spruce and verdant, and worshipped by all.

Young Simon Cheney, though possessed of quite a large share of unpleasant maxims and manners, was certainly set up in Mockery—his red, youthful face puffed and plumed with gross conceit, his light-coloured hair brushed and curled by his hard-worked mother, who continued even when the boy was twenty to tend him at bedtime—as a fine Phallic symbol for the young ladies to admire and for Mr. Caddy to talk about.

Such a god, whose business was pleasure, and whose pleasure was a girl, had waited for Mary upon the hill; and now, when she had let the horse go and went mildly to Simon, he, who had waited a little impatiently for her, having watched her loitering in the lane, at once threw her down upon the grass near to the green mound all amongst the Roddites.

Had Mr. Roddy been watching he would indeed have been sadly disturbed at such a shameless despising of his grand discovery. But Mary not being Mr. Roddy, had only one fear in her mind, and that was that she might see the nakedness of the sky; otherwise she was pleasantly smiling and was never more happy. She shut her eyes, for this garment of darkness can at any moment—and Mary had used it before—become a shield safe against all the elemental nakedness of sea, sky, or man.

'Oh,' gasped Mary, when she was a little recovered from her excitement because of having been thrown down so rudely amongst the Roddites—'Oh, 'tis well the sun be sunk down, for 'e do stare so in daytime.'

God Simon rose lazily from the grass and threw a white chalk stone at the horse who was feeding near by and taking, which was wise of him, no notice of the grassy happenings.

Mary sat up and looked down upon Mockery; she saw all nature—after a little shaking of herself and brushing that she hurriedly completed with fast, ready fingers —there below her now as completely clothed.

It wasn't our pretty god's habit to loiter beside a girl after having amused himself with her, as more ordinary folk would do, leading this aftermath of maidenhood with whispered promises home to her cottage. But Simon, when he had entertained himself for a few moments with stoning the horse, left Mary and strode home along the lane thinking of Dinah Pottle.

Mary didn't mind his going, she was used

to that; and she hung up Dick's halter upon the gate, and looked up at the sky with less timidity now because a decent small cloud in shape like a loin-cloth had crept over it.

Mary, who was blushing and happy, followed Simon Cheney down the lane and watched him enter the large gate and go towards his father's house that stood up finely, beside the large trees that looked sombre and mighty under the darkening sky.

As the milk-cans behind her cottage were nicely garnished and set in a row, Mary Gulliver supposed that her father was resting in his armchair looking, as he always did now of an evening, at the map of the world that had been given to him by Mr. James Tarr.

Mr. Gulliver's ideas of virtue, and the awfulness of any outbreak into nakedness or naked happenings, such as a child that is born to the unmarried, were certainly as strong as his daughter Mary's.

'If anything ever happened,' he would tell her, 'if thee ever did do any of they wicked things that parson did tell we of, 'tis best to drown thee self.'

But though he had such ideas, Mr. Gulliver was born of the softest kind of the Mockery mould. He was one whose feelings were friendly to mild wet days, to lowly cottages, and to mangel-wurzel when snugly housed in the dark end of an old barn.

Mr. Gulliver walked through the days of his life in a friendly manner, nodding at the meal-time hours as if they knew him and nodded back; and he would look at all living and dead things with an affectionate misunderstanding.

Mr. Gulliver had his own notions about great men and great matters. Mr. Cheney he thought too grasping; he honoured Mr. Pattimore; but Mr. Roddy's agent, Mr. Pink, was the man that he really admired.

If Mr. Gulliver ever wondered about the sea, and he used to wonder sometimes, he would go to Mr. Caddy's gate where Mr. Caddy always leaned and ask for information. There he would listen carefully to Mr. Caddy, who would inquire in his turn of the ducks, and the ducks would be sure to quack loud enough —being runners—for Mr. Caddy to explain what they meant.

The wisdom of the ducks would usually show the sea as a very large green beast with a voice, so Mr. Caddy would explain, that exactly resembled that of Farmer Cheney's black bull.

''Tis best to keep out of 'is way, so thik drake do tell I,' Mr. Caddy would remark; 'though of course there be Mr. Pink to go to when the sea do break into the land.'

This allusion to Mr. Pink referred to the kindly habits of the agent, whose mediation in every matter between Mr. Roddy and his tenants was always successful.

Gulliver, though as mild as a Mockery worm, had once turned unexpectedly when Caddy, letting the sea alone for the moment, had spoken of Mary, hinting harmlessly enough that the newest kind of bed, 'where blankets be all green and don't need no making, could be found upon the cliff where wold horse be led to.'

Something then boiled up in Mr. Gulliver, whose daughter's honour was his dearest possession, and who, though most anxious to hear all her merry tales from her own lips—for all tales were far separate from the real in his mind—could never bear the least discrediting hint to come from another.

Mr. Caddy noticed the changed look, and when he knew that Gulliver's fist was waiting pleasantly about an inch from his nose he looked discreetly at the ducks.

'If anything did happen to she, there 'd be a killing,' shouted Mr. Gulliver, waving both his fists around Mr. Caddy as if they were wheels.

Caddy bowed his head. 'They ducks do know,' he said meekly, 'that I never meant no harm. . . .'

When his tea was prepared, Mary went to her father's chair, leaned over him, and looked at the map too. The map was an early picture of the world, drawn in the fine fancy of those ancient times, when the earth was excitingly alive with monsters and devils, that were outside instead of inside folks' minds as they are to-day.

Mr. Gulliver moved his finger over the map and pointed out to Mary a large monster flying over the northern lands.

Mary looked, and carried away by the excitement of the evening she said: 'Something were a-flying over Mockery cliff, where horse were led to, and did flop down upon I, and 'tis most likely 'twere thik, for me eyes were shut.'

'They things oughtn't to be allowed about,' said Mr. Gulliver decidedly.

'Something did throw I down,' continued Mary, who was grown a little paler, perhaps by thinking of such a monster—'something did throw I down, and when I did open my eyes to see who 'twere, there weren't no one, only Simon Cheney who were throwing chalk stones about.'

Mr. Gulliver looked upon his daughter with horror; he believed that something horrible, something depicted in his map, had visited Mary.

'Miss Pink,' he said, 'that do keep lamp burning in she's front room, do tell that a horrible beast out of the wide seas be expected each night-time.'

'Oh,' gasped Mary, 'and that bain't all, for the children do shout and call about the Nellie-bird.'

'You haven't seen nothing more, 'ave 'ee?' asked Mr. Gulliver, looking first at Mary's wide-open eyes and parted lips and then at the map, as if to search for another horror. 'You never see'd nothing else, did 'ee?'

'They wide skies did look at I,' replied Mary, trembling.

''Tain't likely thee did look out to sea, when cows were drove up?'

'Something did rush along dried grass like rats a-running, and then'—and Mary shivered as if the cold horror of it all held her tight—'I did see smoke that rose up out of fisherman's chimney where no one do bide.'

''Tis best we do make hay of thik field,' remarked Mr. Gulliver in a low tone, looking at the window. 'For a field bain't safe for cows where there be fire-drakes.'

Mr. Gulliver slowly moved his finger over his map and pointed out the monster he had named for Mary to see.

''Twouldn't be proper for a poor cow to meet thik,' said Mr. Gulliver.

Chapter 7

A TRUE NELLIE

NO ONE can walk down any pretty lane, that is hung perhaps with garlands of old-man's-beard, without discovering himself after a mile or two in some village or other where fear, that hidden, creeping thing, has sucked out the heart's blood of more than one simple and timid human creature.

Very few villages indeed have escaped Mr. Tarr, whose enterprise and courage even on rainy days would carry him, with or without Miss Ogle and the others, into the most secluded valley, where he would be sure to start many a meek being into looking for impossible wonders, or else trying to prepare themselves for some dread appearance.

Miss Martha Pink, whose brother, with his large wondering face bent over Mr. Roddy's rent books, showed that he wished to do his duty, though his beliefs were elsewhere—Miss Pink, with her tiny nose and her lamp that always burned after sunset in the parlour though she never sat there, was exactly the very appearance for fear to annoy.

Martha Pink, being more timid than wise, had lived her life until Mr. Tarr came with but two thoughts in it, her brother's dinner and her parlour lamp, that showed by its light that she needed a lover.

Mockery understood Miss Pink, for even before Mr. Tarr's visit the extreme restlessness and excitement of the rude children had foretold by their dreadful shouting in the lanes that something was expected.

And now Miss Pink feared the worst. Besides fear, that dread horror, there was also in Mockery the love longing, a matter that when kept silent or buried deep always breaks out in midnight wakefulness, sighs, and aching tears, and which also—for waters must find their level—bubbles up sometimes under pillows and in hidden cupboards.

Perhaps it was partly because of the portrait of the Dean, her relative, the picture that she carried with her to Mockery, that Mr. Pattimore, aged then about fifty-five, married his wife Nellie—or Dorcas, as he re-named her after the honeymoon.

He had taken a holiday in Norfolk, at a rectory where, besides the picture of the Dean, and his old friend the rector and his wife, there was something else too. This was neither the windmill nor the goose green, but a young girl of twenty, the daughter of his friend.

It was on a day when the August sun, heavy with love, covered the green lands with its glory, that Mr. Pattimore pulled her, who was to be his wife, out from the laurel bush.

She had been about the house, as the young

lady must needs be because it was her home, but the portrait of the Dean had been there too, and that—a clear vision of the fine gaiters that his calling might lead him to—had taken all Mr. Pattimore's indoor attention. But this August day, Mr. Pattimore in strolling by noticed something white in the laurel bush beside the drive.

Mr. Pattimore, who knew no more about birds than he did about women—for all his thoughts were with the Apostles—supposed that an owl might be resting there or a white rook, and so he moved the leaves a little aside and peeped in.

He saw no night bird, but a young girl in a white frock pleasantly seated amongst the boughs, and fully as tempting, with her red lips and firm roundness—for Mr. Pattimore's eyes strayed—as any maid since the world cooled. Her hair, not dark but brown enough for darkness, was pleasantly tumbled, so that Mr. Pattimore couldn't help wishing that his fingers were in it, and her blush when she saw his eyes looking at her made the good gentleman glad to remember that he wasn't settled in a Church that forbade marriage.

As soon as Mr. Pattimore heard that the portrait of the Dean, towards which his high hopes lay as soon as he saw it, could go to Mockery as a wedding present with the young lady, he decided to marry her, and so he did.

But Mr. Pattimore had no idea what the laurel bush had done to his chosen. Nellie used to take her book there, and the laurel, a maiden too, would tell her, as soon as she was safely settled, to think about pretty men.

She may have had a fairy story in her mind, when she thought of her lover as a frog who hopped around her looking up with its large eyes asking a question, until it finally hopped into her lap. And after thinking of the man like that, she would think about the baby, and pull leaves from the laurel and pretend to make its clothes. 'My baby,' she would whisper to herself every time now that she climbed into the bush, until Mr. Pattimore with the frog's manners pulled her out, his hands a little more wantonly inclined than a clergyman's should be.

The Dean—not the portrait this time, but the carnal man—wrote to Nellie, as soon as she was safely at Mockery and the picture hung up and the honeymoon over, and Mr. Pattimore read the letter as proudly as if he had written it himself.

The Dean said, 'Remember St. Paul.'

'He must have meant me,' said Mr. Patti-more, 'when he said that.'

Mr. Pattimore began to take cold baths.

But that wasn't the worst.

He now saw all women, his young wife included, as wholesale temptations to wanton naughtiness. . . . Two nights after the return from the honeymoon, Mr. Pattimore stared for a full half-hour about bedtime at the picture, and fled to the attic.

Mrs. Pattimore lay that night, in the pretty bedroom upon which so much money had been spent, alone and in tears.

Her husband appeared the next day in a black garment that reached to his toes. He talked only at breakfast about the proposed sewing meeting, and Mrs. Pattimore could think only about the frog.

When he asked her to pass the toast, he said: 'The toast, please, Dorcas.'

And Mrs. Pattimore, her eyes still dim with her night's crying, exclaimed, 'But I'm Nellie, you know—darling Nellie.'

'You're Dorcas now,' replied her husband sternly.

Mrs. Pattimore had been a little proud of the Dean too—he was her second cousin on her mother's side—in bygone times, but now she could never look up at the picture without feeling what a great harm the Dean had done to her when he mentioned St. Paul in the wedding letter. 'Cousin Ashbourne might have talked to him at the wedding instead of writing when that was over,' she used to say sadly; 'he wouldn't have listened to him then.'

Nellie Pattimore, changed now to a Dorcas, was as meek as a dove and just as loving. She would sit up in her bed in all her night finery and pout a little because he wasn't there; and though there didn't seem to be the least hope of a baby coming, she couldn't help imagining there might be, and was beginning to sew some tiny garments. She began with a christening gown, and as soon as she was sure that she couldn't have a baby she tried to pretend that she was making the gown for some other mother's little one; though she could hardly bear to think, for she so longed herself, that there were other mothers in the world.

As each spring-time came—and Dorcas had only been married five years when Mr. Tarr and Miss Ogle invaded the village—she would comfort herself with the flowers, calling them all, when no one heard, 'her pretty babies,' because when she knelt down upon a soft mossy bank to smell a cowslip she felt sure that the scent of a real baby's neck would be just like that.

Mrs. Pattimore lived at Mockery harm-lessly enough with her longing that hid itself in her feelings for the flowers and in the bed-room wardrobe where she kept her sewing. She would listen meekly enough when Mr. Pattimore, with eyes fixed upon the hard, stupid lines of the Dean's—'dear Cousin Ashbourne'—face, would speak more to the picture than to her, and tell him how Caddy—that lazy Caddy!—corrupted all the youth of Mockery with his nasty conversations that he

always addressed to the ducks—as Mr. Pattimore did his to the Dean.

'He sets all their hearts and minds,' said
Mr. Pattimore one April day at lunch, 'agape
for all naughtiness.'

Mrs. Pattimore blushed and looked down;
she felt—and so many women have felt the
same—that if all his outcry against wantonness could only be changed by the grand trump
of love, what a lover he would become—and
then the baby!

A few moments after lunch Mrs. Pattimore
peeped into the dining-room, dressed to go
out, just to see what he was doing.

Mr. Pattimore, with his hands clasped and
his face a sad one, in which pride and hatred
of sin were coupled, still stared at the Dean.

Mrs. Pattimore, with thoughts as hasty as
a young girl's who means to be naughty,
hurried out of the house to ask a question of
Mr. Caddy. She found Miss Pink, with her
large scarf of grey wool that certainly any of
Mrs. Gaskell's Cranford ladies would have
taken, as we have done, for a shawl, standing
beside the churchyard gate waiting for Mr.
Pink, who had for some reason or other entered
the edifice of one hundred and eighty-two
sittings.

'Have you seen Mr. Caddy?' inquired
Mrs. Pattimore of Miss Pink. 'I want to
ask him something.'

'Oh yes,' replied Miss Pink, speaking out of the folds of her shawl; 'he's leaning over his cottage gate and talking to the ducks as usual.'

And so he was; but when Dorcas came near to him, wishing to learn the right path to naughtiness that she hoped would help her to her husband's love, instead of going on telling the ducks and Mary Gulliver, who now modestly withdrew, about the leg of a bedstead, that astonished the late wedding guests taking their last cups by coming through the ceiling, he said to Mrs. Pattimore, 'Mockery be a fine place for summer roses to grow in.'

'But it isn't time for the roses yet, Mr. Caddy,' said the lady, her blush becoming an ordinary look of disappointment.

'They little small flowers be so pretty,' remarked Mr. Caddy, looking into the meadows. 'They do always hear what God be a-saying when it do rain.'

'But, Mr. Caddy'—Mrs. Pattimore looked after the departing form of Mary; she meant to make her plunge—'a pretty girl likes to——'

'To gather a flower for poor mother's grave.' Mr. Caddy looked sadly at the churchyard.

A loud clamour came near—the Mockery children; they were chasing a black cat up the lane with shouts and stones. They were led by Esther, who called out to Mr. Caddy that the cat was soon to have kittens, and ran on shouting.

Mrs. Pattimore looked around Mockery. She wished to comment upon something that would set Mr. Caddy off talking to the ducks again.

In the middle of a wide field she saw Mrs. Topple going from one part of the field to another, stooping down and looking.

'Poor 'oman,' said Mr. Caddy, seeing her too; 'she do spend all her time in looking for good-luck clover.'

The tall, drooping figure of Mr. Pink came out of the little shop; he walked carefully down the stone path and then down the lane in the direction of his house.

''E do try to get Mrs. Moggs to go to the beautiful sea,' explained Mr. Caddy when Mr. Pink had departed; 'but she do only ring they bells and smile at 'e.'

Miss Pink now came near, hurrying from the churchyard as if frightened; she had missed Mr. Pink, who had left the church by another path. Miss Pink begged Mrs. Pattimore to take her home.

'My brother only thinks of saving Mrs. Moggs' soul now,' she said. 'And something's been seen in the sea.'

'They children do tell of a Nellie-bird,' said Mr. Caddy.

Mrs. Pattimore turned sadly away with Miss

Pink; she had learned nothing from Mr. Caddy.

But when she was gone, though not quite out of hearing, Mr. Caddy said, turning to the duck-pond:

''Tis a pretty petticoat that do do it, so Mary do say, and a pair of white stockings.'

Mrs. Pattimore hardly listened to Miss Pink, who was telling her that she believed the beast of the Book of Revelation and the Nellie-bird the children told of were one and the same.

Chapter 8

'ONE OF THEY PRINGS'

IT was the first of May. The Mockery cliff was white with the daisies that the ignorant and simple-minded will always admire—leaving the Roddites unnoticed.

Though the sun had shone sometimes since Miss Ogle had visited the village, soft rain-clouds had, more often than the sun, covered Mockery in a sweet warm garment that now gave a fine greenness to the grass and opened the daisies.

Mrs. Pattimore was so taken with the morning and with the pleasant thought that cowslips were abroad, that she couldn't help looking into the dining-room—where Mr. Pattimore always wrote his sermons in order to be near to the Dean—to see how busy he was, as she often used to.

He was busy, for his text, written large upon a page of foolscap—'But this I say, brethren, the time is short; it remaineth, that both they that have wives be as though they had none'—would, she felt, as she closed the door again without speaking, keep him so for many an hour. Mrs. Pattimore went out with a sigh.

Mrs. Pattimore wore a grey knitted coat, and when she stood in front of the Mockery vicarage—a pretty creature who longed for her mate—she felt the sun warm and press her like a god on fire. In the lane the sun was still warmer. Mrs. Pattimore looked over a gate at Farmer Cheney's barns and meadows.

A white cock with shining, fluttering wings, intent upon amorous adventure, chased a pretty black hen; and a bull and a ram in the same field were both busy and playful.

Mrs. Pattimore knelt upon the soft grass of the bank and smelt a daisy. She wished that she had never been taken out of the laurel bush in Norfolk and had continued all her life thinking about the frog. She now knew that she couldn't dream any more, but could only long.

All Mockery was there, and all Mockery was intent upon doing something or other.

James Pring, the mender of the Mockery roads, was standing with his spade over his shoulder before his cottage door. He was looking at the address upon an envelope that he had taken out of his pocket, evidently intending to carry the letter to its proper destination, though not at once, for he put it into his pocket again.

There came a scream from Mr. Cheney's rick-yard, and Rebecca Pring, the girl who worked as a daily servant at the vicarage, ran round one haystack and then round another, followed by the gay Simon, whose coat fluttered and shone like the cock's wing in the sun.

Dorcas Pattimore saw all Mockery happy and gay, and she couldn't help trembling, because she wished so much to be happy too.

The larks sang, the magpies chattered, and the little wrens hopped about in the ivy without saying a word about the nest hidden in that very bank.

Mary Gulliver came by with her father's lunch; she was exactly the proper fair, pretty maid to be there—'and no doubt Simon runs after her too,' thought Mrs. Pattimore, 'and Mr. Caddy had mentioned a petticoat, and Mary wore white stockings.' There was plenty of roundness about Mary, plenty of young girlhood to take hold of in the sight of the sun. Mary wore no hat, and the sun lit up her hair that tended to gold, so that Mrs. Pattimore, with her heart so dreadfully set on fire, wished that she were either Mary Gulliver or at the worst a ewe or a hen. And Mr. Caddy had told her nothing.

Mary passed demurely. She knew as much as Mrs. Pattimore did about the attic, the wedding bed deserted by the stern man, and about the little garments in the wardrobe.

Mary looked at Mrs. Pattimore with pity as she went by.

Others came by too—the Mockery children out to play; they were chasing the rooks, that fortunately were out of their reach, and were shouting as they went by, 'The Nellie-bird do live in fisherman's hut; 'e be a-come; thik nasty thing be a-come!'

The heart of Dorcas beat violently, partly

because of the rude noise that the children were making, and partly because she had meant that very morning to go down to the sea.

She started to go a little hesitatingly, not knowing what the children had meant by their strange shout, and remembering too how Miss Pink had spoken about the beast and the Nellie-bird.

Going beside Mrs. Pottle's cottage—the nearest way to the sea—Mrs. Pattimore saw that lady surrounded by a litter of kittens, who raised their blind heads and squirmed in the path while Mrs. Pottle stood over them like a fierce giant.

The mother cat had escaped the children who had chased it some days before, and had safely produced its young that Mrs. Pottle had now strewed in the path after shutting up the mother in her wood-shed.

The blind kittens raised their heads in order to ask pity from a world that to them was a mere place of murder, with the murderess Mrs. Pottle standing above and ready to beat them to death with a great stick.

'You be Mrs. Pring,' she shouted, beginning to lay about her with the stick. And when she hit a kitten she yelled the louder—for Mrs. Pring's cottage was so near—'You be Mrs. Pring that I be killing.'

As soon as Mrs. Pottle had killed them all,

she smiled at Mrs. Pattimore, who had looked on horrified at the slaughter. Mrs. Pottle's smile—a reddened one, for the blood of a kitten had spotted her cheek—was but meant to hold Mrs. Pattimore a moment.

Dorcas looked at her in horror when she said in a loud, angry tone, 'Bain't we got a marble clock wi' hands that go round and round after they figures?'

Mrs. Pottle looked across at the Prings' cottage with the scorn of one who has a possession worth all her enemies.

'What have they Prings got?' she shouted, looking fiercely at Dorcas, who was trembling again.

Mrs. Pattimore, who was cowed by the woman, really thought that she wished to know; and so she replied, harmlessly enough: 'Mrs. Pring has a lame cow, a few black hens, and a pig that has some—' Mrs. Pattimore hesitated and blushed—'little baby ones.'

Mrs. Pottle looked down at the path. 'Bain't we got cats and kittens?' she exclaimed angrily.

Mrs. Pattimore looked at the kittens; there was a little life still in one of them, that Mrs. Pottle was now kind enough to squash out of it with her heavy heel. 'One of they Prings,' she said as she did so.

Chapter 9

LED BY THE FLOWERS

As soon as Mrs. Pattimore left Mrs. Pottle's cottage gate, inside of which the dead kittens lay, she walked quickly, and, hardly noticing where she was going, she went down the lane towards the sea.

'I know I shouldn't do this,' she said to herself, 'and I should go home.' She caught a mind's glimpse in a moment of time of Rebecca Pring.

Rebecca was a pleasant and friendly creature with nice manners, and with feelings that loved all men, and especially clergymen. Though, because Mr. Pattimore would say so little to her, she had learned to look more than she should perhaps have done at the portrait of the Dean.

Rebecca would often declare that gaiters were very becoming to a man; and that she had taken service with Mr. Pattimore—a daily service—only because she had heard of the portrait and its fine legs.

Rebecca, the vicar's lady knew, would be now more likely watching at the back door for God Simon, a proper one to mention the clergy to, than watching the behaviour of the mutton in the oven.

But that could not be helped now, for Dorcas Pattimore had peeped over a stile and had seen cowslips that grew all along the path to the seashore. The Mockery brook, too, that bubbled over the clean white pebbles, went the same road, and beside it there were primroses.

Mrs. Pattimore paused beside the stile for one moment. Shouts of 'The Nellie-bird be come!' came from the village.

Mrs. Pattimore climbed over the stile. Nearly every one, and certainly a pretty lady who feels warm May longings flutter within her, catches a kind of wanton excitement as she approaches the sea. Even though her home be but half a mile away, the feeling of the sea, the great and little fishes, the seaweed, the rocks, the white foam, and the ships poised upon its naked spaces, all raise in the human heart the excitement and expectation of love.

The wide waste of waters sings and cries to all, making the heart beat faster, as though something at least will be seen or heard of down there that will inspire all life with a fine hope and joyfulness.

The cowslips led Mrs. Pattimore; she couldn't hold back with so many flowers wishing her to come. All lovely things met her; she opened her arms, and the soft wind laden with delicious scent embraced her. She felt rich and fruitful; the kind wind had pressed and crept about her, and she knew the joy of conception.

She reached a green bank that was almost beside the sea, where large cowslips grew upon long, firm stalks. She looked down upon them with eyes moist and ready for love, and the cowslips returned her look with yellow wavings.

'Even the flowers want me to lie down,' thought Mrs. Pattimore, who now lay down upon the green bank that was so pleasantly warmed by the May sunshine.

Mrs. Pattimore had never seen the sea in the same way as the people of Mockery regarded it, as a moving field, not so pleasant as Mr. Gulliver's, and certainly not so safe to look at. But their fears, with that shout of 'the Nellie-bird,' had at least got to her and frightened her. She was alone amid the tall cowslips, and she didn't like to look at the sea.

Instead of looking, she lay with her hands in her lap allowing the hot sun to soak into her. 'Had God Simon'—and she had more than once thought of his simple manners as godlike—'ever brought Dinah Pottle'—Mrs Pattimore saw her then—'just to that spot where she now lay so ready for love?' Dinah as round as an orange and as ripe, and such a girl! She was so much of a girl that even Mr. Cheney's bull would wander after her in all friendliness, mistaking her apparently for another Europa. Even Mr. Pattimore when Dinah passed him would be forced to clench his teeth and think of the Dean's gaiters in order to prevent himself from making a sound like a neigh.

Dinah, of course, was very willing to be with God Simon, 'changing even gates and hurdles and rough faggots into bedsteads'; so Mr. Caddy would inform his ducks, and saying, 'Well, there, she be so rounded that she don't feel nothing.'

'Oh, but I am alone,' whispered Mrs. Pattimore to herself, picking a tall cowslip with a firm stalk, 'and I wish this cowslip were my dear husband—but oh, that Dean!'

Forgetting her fears in her wish, Mrs. Pattimore looked at the sea. She sat up, though she still leaned against the bank, and she stretched out her arms to the sea. Something was singing in the sea.

Her fancy and excitement were so alive that she fancied the song must be about her, and that a young man was singing, or perhaps the Nellie-bird.

Mrs. Pattimore trembled. 'There were large fishes in the sea, mermen perhaps?' she thought, 'and of course they were fine singers. It couldn't be that horrid beast that Miss Pink talked about; no, the singing was strong and full—a man's.'

She listened entranced.

Her father had read to her, when she was a little girl and had hardly learned the way into the laurel bush, out of an old brown and worm-eaten book that told how a swan had once loved a maiden.

'Perhaps that swan was also a kind of Nellie-bird—but the voice must be a man's, it was so full and joyous.'

Mrs. Pattimore started; she had allowed one of her hands to rest upon the warm grass, and she now took it hurriedly away. A snake had moved under her hand. The snake crawled into the grass; it hadn't bitten her. Mrs. Pattimore didn't jump up at once; although it had frightened her, she didn't seem to mind this snake; and now that it had crawled away into the grass without hurting her, she rather liked the idea of it.

But what were those cows of Mr. Gulliver's looking at?—a boat? Yes, and more than a boat, for there was a man in it.

A man—Mrs. Pattimore looked at him longingly; he was standing in the boat holding to the mast, and letting the boat drift with the tide; he looked free and happy.

Mrs. Pattimore knew the man from the children's description of him; he was the new fisherman—the Nellie-bird.

Chapter 10

MRS. PATTIMORE IS LATE FOR DINNER

THE adventurous fisherman named John Dobbin who had once tried to do business with the Mockery seas had failed. He had built a small hut in a low and sheltered corner, in in which he lived within a yard or two of the creeping ripples of the high tides.

John Dobbin who had once been a simple gardener and worked for Mr. Tarr, who, wishing perhaps to get rid of the man, had told him of all the mackerel, crabs, prawns, and whiting—enough to make any man rich—that swam or crawled in the bay of Mockery Gap. John soon discovered the sea to be a very rude and unmanageable garden, with waves that broke his lobster-pots, near drowned himself, and beat in all one side of his new boat. And so he took the few things that he possessed, together with one live creature that had come to him out of the sea, and, leaving the boat behind and the hut, for Mr. Gulliver's light spring waggon couldn't carry them, Mr. Dobbin returned to Maidenbridge and obtained work at the cemetery, an employment that soothed his troubled mind.

No fisherman had come to Mockery since Mr. Dobbin until he whom Mrs. Pattimore now watched drifting past her and going towards the little hollow in the low cliffs where the hut was.

Mrs. Pattimore ate him with her eyes. He was tall, and his hair, curly and light-coloured, glistened like yellow guineas. His beard, yellow too, and finely coloured—and Mrs. Pattimore never even wondered why he hadn't a cap—expressed a fine and idle recklessness that accorded well with the way that he drifted and sang his song. The man's strength showed plainly enough in his fine limbs, and the careless manner of his standing told of one who cared more for life than for meat, and more for the body than for raiment.

The boat drifted near to the hut, and the fisherman with a careless thrust of an oar sent her to land. As he leapt out in a light manner, the sun shone so upon his yellow hair that it appeared to Mrs. Pattimore to be a crown of gold.

The excitement of Mrs. Pattimore's feelings had prevented her from noticing that others watched too—Mr. Gulliver's cows. These cows were standing quite near to her, and were watching the boat with the same interest as herself.

Mrs. Pattimore went a little aside and climbed a soft, grassy mound. Around her and sprouting out from the ground was a forest of mare's-tail. These minutely-made trees, that bear so strong a resemblance to real

ones, Mrs. Pattimore seemed to notice for the
first time in her life, and she supposed that
they, like herself, had been surprised by the
exciting vision of the new fisherman.

But she couldn't stand there for ever, even
though the sun and the cowslips might wish
to keep her; for as it was Rebecca and not
Dinah that Master Simon the fine young god
of Mockery was after that day, the mutton
would grow black in the oven while Rebecca . . .
Mrs. Pattimore had once noticed something
odd happening in the corner of the vicarage
garden. And also—Mrs. Pattimore didn't dare
to look at the sea again—something must have
happened to the time of day too, as well as—
which was very likely—to the vicarage cooking.
For coming towards her was Mary Gulliver,
walking fast as though she were late, to fetch
up the cows.

Mrs. Pattimore hurried to the stile. But
even with her fears for the dinner she had to
stop there, because she heard Mr. Pink and
Farmer Cheney talking in the lane, and she
didn't wish to rudely interrupt them by her
presence—and so Dorcas waited.

The two men were standing under the shade
of a tall elm tree in the lane, and Farmer
Cheney, with his unbuttoned beard shaking,
was looking up into the meek, wide face of
Mr. Pink, whose old straw hat was perched
like a queer bird at the extreme back of his

head, and saying angrily, 'You allow all the thieves in the world to come to Mockery; there's the schoolmistress who's always spying about in my fields, and now there's this fisherman, who will want to know what I be looking for when I do dig in Cliff mound.'

'But what are you digging for?' replied Mr. Pink, trying to turn away Mr. Cheney's wrath with a mild question.

'Rabbits,' said Mr. Cheney.

Mrs. Pattimore blushed; she didn't like to listen, and yet she couldn't climb over the stile, for, besides the rudeness of breaking in upon the men, they might watch her climbing!

'And there's Gulliver,' called out the farmer loudly, 'who you allow to go on year after year without paying his rent, and who talks only of monsters; he's little better than a thief to landlord.'

'Mr. Gulliver,' said Mr. Pink, in the tone of voice that he used when any one's faults were mentioned—'Mr. Gulliver is interested in geography.'

'So 'e mid be,' exclaimed the farmer. 'And suppose new fisherman be interested in maidens, me boy Simon, that I've a-worked all me life for together wi' 'is own mother, will kick and scream in's bed for sadness.'

'But there are quite a number of young women in Mockery, and there's Mrs. . . .'

Mrs. Pattimore climbed over the stile.

Farmer Cheney turned away, and Mr. Pink met her with his usual question, 'Had she noticed Mrs. Moggs going to the sea?'

Mrs. Pattimore blushed, and replied that she hadn't.

'What can I give,' asked Mr. Pink, 'to poor Mrs. Moggs, whose bells only ring when she's happy, and who's never seen the sea? Isn't there any pretty thing that I can give her? for one lovely thing, Mrs. Pattimore, you know, leads to another.'

Mrs. Pattimore wanted to go, but she liked Mr. Pink, and she wished to say something; a tiny mouse rustled the ivy in the hedge and darted up the bank.

'I used to keep white mice when I was a girl,' she said.

Mr. Pink rubbed his hands joyfully.

'The very thing Mr. Tarr advised,' he said.

Mrs. Pattimore entered the vicarage by the front door at almost the same moment that Rebecca Pring entered, coming from her favourite corner of the garden, at the back.

Rebecca blushingly met her mistress and rang the dinner-bell.

Chapter 11

AN UGLY THING

WE fancy ourselves as wise as the old gentleman who holds up his hands and points to heaven and its amusements that await the good.

We hold out our hands too and show the world Mockery Gap, and point out that there are pretty pebbles to pick up along the sea-shore.

Pebbles, that from the point of view of the Author of all things—and bow to Him we had better, or we may rue the omission—may as well be looked at as anything else that He has made. All life is but a looking, so why not stare at Mr. Roddy? and if gentility is a little dull sometimes, there is Dinah Pottle only now gone in under those fine trees of Mockery wood, where a church once used to be, the oldest in the country.

This wood—the very one where the hermit prayed, the same who rowed out to save the ancient mariner when the young fisher-boy went out of his wits—goes down to the sea, or at least as near to the sea as it can conveniently get without being uprooted by the waves.

God Simon, that fine bird, had followed pretty Dinah—'an' thik wood be she's bed,' as Mr. Caddy had often informed Mary

83

Gulliver, adding too that the green mound upon
Mockery cliff was as soft as they fir cones,
not to mention the sunny side of a garden
hedge or a straw stack—the one near the
vicarage—where Master Simon would meet
Rebecca.

Mr. Gulliver, whose eyes were always search-
ing for strange monsters, often looked at the
Mockery wood, and sometimes saw two figures
go in and only one come out, for it was Simon
Cheney's custom to at once return home after
an adventure in order to brag to his parents
how finely he had used the girl.

Every one in this pretty world wishes to
put every one else right in his doings, whether
good or ill.

For even Mrs. Topple would look upon
herself as upon another person, and would
hunt for her prize of a large clover with a fine
zeal in order to cure this other person of her
lameness.

Mr. Pink, of course, believed—and he
would now go about and inquire of every one,
'Who sold white mice?'—that if Mrs. Moggs
went once to the sea, she would not only be
saved herself, but the whole world would be
saved in her salvation.

'Her soul must feel sorrowful,' Mr. Pink
would remark to his sister, whose little nose
appeared to be growing smaller than ever;
'it must long to get away at least for an hour

84

or two from so many balls of string and pen-wipers.'

Mr. Pink liked to go to the Mockery shop, stepping carefully upon the stone path to avoid the cracks, and he would say, after paying for the stamps, which he always remembered to do, 'You ought to go and look at the beautiful sea, Mrs. Moggs.'

'Oh, it's quite enough for me,' Mrs. Moggs would reply, ringing her bells happily, 'to hear the waves roar, so I have no wish to go and look at them.'

Sometimes Mr. Pink, every inch of his wide face glowing with hope for Mrs. Moggs' salvation, would describe the Mockery sea. 'It's as beautiful as the blue sky,' he would say; 'its colours are as deep and wonderful as itself, and are like'—and Mr. Pink would look excitedly around him—'those pretty sweets on your top shelf, Mrs. Moggs.'

'But it's a long way to the sea,' and the postmistress would sigh.

'Only half a mile,' Mr. Pink would reply.

'But then Mr. Hunt might find some one in the shop taking the postal orders,' and Mrs. Moggs' bells would stop ringing and she would look very sad.

Nearly every day, except when the rude brats the Mockery children clamoured for sweets, Mrs. Moggs' kindly face would glow with content; but a day would come sometimes when she looked timid and careworn, and this always happened when Mr. Hunt, the postmaster from the town, rudely pushed open the shop door and came in with his questions. His questions were always about the money, and he would look hard at Mrs. Moggs as he questioned her, as though he were sure that she had done something with the stamps or the orders that she shouldn't have done.

'If ever you allow any one to owe you for a stamp you'll get yourself into trouble,' Mr. Hunt the postmaster would say crossly.

Mrs. Moggs would look timidly into the face of her inquisitor, as if she fully expected him to tell her the very next moment to go to the workhouse, a place that was in Mrs. Moggs' idea the very nearest thing in England to a torture chamber.

Sometimes when Mr. Hunt had brought Mrs. Moggs almost to tears, and the happy ringing of her bells to a sad silence, the post-master would ask in a fine breezy way, copied exactly from Mr. James Tarr, as he stretched out his stockinged legs in imitation of the same personage, 'How far off was the sea?'

'Oh, Mr. Pink is always talking about the sea,' Mrs. Moggs would reply nervously, 'but I have never been there, you know.'

Whenever Mrs. Moggs had a bad dream it would always take the form of some loss or other connected with the stamps or the postal orders. And in the winter nights, when the wind shook the ivy outside the window, or when in autumn the great red harvest moon peeped through her curtains, she would wake in terror hearing Mr. Hunt, in the grand bullying voice that he always used to inferiors, telling her, who was the kindest old woman in the world, that she was a thief and a liar.

She didn't mind the thief much, for she remembered one, although Mr. Pattimore had never said much about him, who once died in God's company with a sure promise of Paradise; but she couldn't bear the thought of being called a liar.

Mr. Hunt would always shout out that word so loudly in her dream, that Mrs. Moggs would awake all trembling, and she would be forced to think of all the fine things Mr. Pink had said about the sea in order to compose herself to sleep again.

And it wasn't only Mrs. Moggs who didn't like Mr. Hunt and his ways, for James Pring, who, together with his lame cow, his wife and family, was hated by Mrs. Pottle, couldn't speak of Mr. Hunt except with disapproval, and he was always glad to remember that Mr. Caddy, the story-teller of Mockery, disliked Mr. Hunt too.

And here we must pause for a moment, and with willing eyes look at pretty Esther Pottle, who, with her hair that hung black all over her, lay naughtily upon the bank to let simple Mr. Pink see her, who, being short-sighted, fancied that she was Mrs. Pattimore, blushed, and went by.

But Mr. Pattimore coming by too, having all the hatred in his heart for the summer manners of rock flies and young ladies, looked and cried out, 'Why, Esther!'

Esther kicked up her legs.

'Esther!' said Mr. Pattimore again, and Esther ran off calling out that the Nellie-bird had come and that Mr. Pattimore wasn't a man at all but an 'old silly.'

Mr. Pattimore shut his eyes.

He thought of his wife. 'Dorcas,' he said sternly as if to pull himself up, in case his legs wished to run after Esther—'Dorcas.'

Chapter 12

GODFATHER PATTIMORE

BEFORE he peeped into the laurel bush and carried off the young creature who became his wife, together with the picture of the Dean that filled all his mind with high hopes, Mr. Pattimore had lived in Mockery some twenty-five years, with Mrs. Topple, who afterwards became the schoolmistress, as his housekeeper.

All that twenty-five years Mr. Pattimore had studied carefully the philosophy of names. And wishing to make this same study a practical help and use to the world, he had, by the simple means of becoming godfather to them all, named the babies of Mockery Gap.

Mr. Pattimore believed in Bible names, 'that cast,' he would say, 'a fine odour of sanctity over the bearers; and, though sinners as we all are, what Peter, Paul, or Simon ever died in his sins?'

Amongst all whom he had stood godfather to, Mr. Pattimore was the most interested in Simon Cheney. He had watched the young man's behaviour from a child. In his study, when Mr. Pattimore wasn't looking at the Dean, and thinking of himself as one, he would look out of either of the two large windows, that showed different views. He would watch for Simon, and he would sometimes see him; he would watch too for Rebecca, for Dinah, and for Mary. Mary wasn't plain Mary to Mr. Pattimore: she was 'the other Mary,' because Mr. Pattimore liked a mystery, and the other Mary surrounds herself with one. Besides, he had named two Marys already after the more important ones in the Bible, but both these had the good or ill fortune—as one likes to take it—of dying of whooping-cough.

He preached about Mr. Gulliver's daughter the Sunday of her christening, explaining that though we hear very little about the other Mary in the Holy Book, she must have been very good and very plain. 'This little one will not be beautiful, but she will be good,' said Mr. Pattimore.

As soon as Mary Gulliver could run, the Mockery children, a sad and naughty crew, would run after her and call out, 'You bain't nothing, you be only t' other maiden.'

Mr. Pattimore had faith in his Simon, who of course was Peter too, the first name of the Keeper of the Keys being to Mr. Pattimore the best to be called by.

When he looked out of the window—he would turn away if Mrs. Pattimore passed by— Mr. Pattimore would sometimes see Rebecca running round the vicarage garden or Mr. Cheney's rick-yard that was near by, having left the vicarage kitchen for a minute or two, and being followed by Simon.

What happened behind the hedge if Simon caught her Mr. Pattimore wished the Dean would tell, but the Dean would only look sternly out of his frame at the half-written sermon upon the gentleman's table.

From the same window, too, Mr. Pattimore would sometimes notice of an evening a spot of colour upon or near to the green mound of Mockery cliff. This colour would reveal itself to Mr. Pattimore as the other Mary. But sometimes she would appear to be over-shadowed by something more drab and common than her own pretty frock could ever be, and Mr. Pattimore would soon notice a figure near to her that appeared to be Master Simon's.

And again, too, at the other window, from which the Mockery wood could be seen as well as the sea, Dinah might be noticed going to the wood for sticks, as she often did—but not always alone, for Dinah's nature was both free and loving, and even Mrs. Topple would rise up from her knees in the field where she had been looking and not praying, and watch for her return; for Dinah would sometimes run out of the wood laughing.

Having seen so much and so far, Mr. Pattimore, the very afternoon of the day when his wife had been led down to the sea by the pretty cowslips and had watched the fisherman near to Mr. Gulliver's cows, decided to go to the Cheneys and at least to ask, not perhaps

what heavenly doors Master Simon had been
unlocking with his keys, but at least whether
he was as good a boy as his name should have
made him.

Mr. Pattimore approached the Cheney abode
with quick steps. The house, a fine tall one,
four hundred years old, and the ancient manor
of the Roddys when the family lived upon their
own lands, stood in the midst of the Mockery
valley among its barns and out-buildings.

Mr. Pattimore never looked at what he
walked upon. Flowers he supposed grew in
Mockery as well as grass and babies. He had
named the babies, and they should all have
grown up as good as their names.

'Dinah!' Yes, but then the Bible maiden
had gone into no wood with Simon Peter;
though even she hadn't been altogether good.

A pleasant path it was that Mr. Pattimore
walked in, a pleasant path, with the afternoon sun
and the fair haze of summer warming all things
about him. But he, with the fine idea of being
akin to a Dean, and of even taking his place one
day though he hadn't an aunt in a king's palace,
brought and kept for ever these thoughts of
grander things than mere buttercups.

But even he with such fine thoughts decided
that he couldn't stay for all the rest of his life
at Mr. Cheney's front door, which, after the
proper habit and custom of all farmhouses,
was securely bolted, and the ringing of the bell

was of no more use than would have been the pulling at the ivy that hung beside the door, except perhaps to shake out the earwigs.

Mr. Pattimore looked at his watch—it had been his father's; he rang the bell at regular intervals for a quarter of an hour, and then, seeing that the door was as firmly bolted as ever, he walked along beside the wall to find another entrance.

The side wall of Mockery Manor had been warmed all the afternoon by the summer sun; but it was neither the warmth of the wall nor the delightful feeling of summer happiness that clings to old country-houses that caused Mr. Pattimore to stop in the path, but simply the mention from inside a window of his own name.

'Caddy do say'—and the voice appeared to be none other than Simon's own—'that Mr. Pattimore bain't no good at bedtime.'

Mr. Pattimore didn't wish to listen, and yet he waited. A moment had come to him, one of those moments when even a good man doesn't know what he ought to do; for he couldn't help noticing, because he had eyes, that Mr. Cheney, with his wife, a wizened, unlovely creature, just behind him, was crossing the fields and going in the direction of the Mockery cliff with pickaxe and spade.

Mr. Pattimore hadn't named them; if he had, perhaps they would have been less likely to listen to Mr. James Tarr. But he had named Simon, and so he couldn't help thinking it right and proper, considering how long he had rung the bell, to wait a little where he was.

Mr. Pattimore touched the wall; he found that it was warm.

For some odd reason that we cannot explain Mr. Pattimore wished that the wall was an iceberg.

"Tain't we maidens that do want what Mr. Caddy do talk of; 'tis poor Mrs. Pattimore.'

The voice and the laugh were Dinah's. 'Rebecca be the one to know what wold Caddy do tell they ducks about,' and Dinah laughed loudly.

Mr. Pattimore leant against the wall, but, try as he would to imagine it cold, he couldn't help feeling fully conscious that the wall was warm. He looked down at the pebbles in the path. They had been brought from the sea, and he supposed that they were warm too.

Mr. Pattimore looked towards the sea; the sun was hot upon it, and the waters afar off glittered and shone.

In the Mockery bay a boat was sailing amid the shining happiness of the waves; the boat shone too, as painted a thing as ever a poet wrote of in prose or song.

At a little distance from the sea a lonely figure was bending over the earth—Mrs. Topple. From the village a cry came, as unreal to a human ear as any summer cry could be—'The Nellie-bird, the Nellie-bird!'

'I must not stay a moment longer,' thought Mr. Pattimore; 'but perhaps it's only that Rebecca has come to tell Simon and her friends about the picture of the Dean.'

And so she had.

''Tain't from Simon'—Rebecca's voice grew serious—'that do practice 'is funny games wi' we maids, that I've learned so much, nor 'tain't from Mr. Caddy's talking to 'is ducks; but 'tis the picture of Dean Ashbourne that do tell of things.'

Mr. Pattimore made a slight sound in his throat. He listened intently.

'Sure 'e don't come out of picture frame to cuddle 'ee,' exclaimed Mary, 'when 'ee be doing fire-grate?'

'No, 'e don't never come out,' replied Rebecca; 'but all same I do look up at 'e and ask questions.'

'And what do they gaiters tell of?' asked Simon, sniggering.

'More than ever they ducks of Mr. Caddy do listen to,' replied Rebecca, amid general laughter.

'His legs be plimmed out with wickedness,' remarked Dinah, who had stared hard at the portrait during the last work-party at the vicarage.

'They bain't made for trousers,' said Rebecca mysteriously. ''E did tell I about they gaiters, and 'e do like to talk too of a maiden's clothes, for they clergy do know.'

Sounds now came through the window, and reached the sun-heated wall against which Mr. Pattimore leaned, which showed that Simon, however saintly his name, could cause amusement.

The queer sound in Mr. Pattimore's throat burst; he coughed. . . .

A moment later all that he had heard faded and went. Mockery Manor became a warmed summer silence. A girl, demure and modest —Rebecca—walked from the farm with a milk-jug in her hand, stepping in the same path by which Mr. Pattimore had arrived, and going towards the vicarage with the evening supply of milk.

A moment later Mary Gulliver, with the hay-knife that she had borrowed from the farm, climbed the stile and disappeared into the lane that led to her home. Mr. Pattimore looked away from her and towards the wood. Dinah was there, walking gladly in under the dark trees and carrying the bag that she usually brought for stick gathering.

Mr. Pattimore peeped into the window from whence the voices had issued.

The room was empty.

Again Mr. Pattimore raised his eyes and looked at the sea and at the wood. Some one followed Dinah in under the trees. This was Simon, the pet god of the Mockery girls.

Mr. Pattimore returned home sadly; he wished to ask Dean Ashbourne a question too.

Chapter 13

MISS PINK FEARS THAT SOMETHING IS COMING

No ONE in Mockery, if we except Mr. Pattimore, was more anxious than Miss Pink to see the new fisherman.

She told her brother that she hoped the fisherman would drive away from that part of the coast the horrid beast that Mr. Tarr had spoken of.

'The children,' she said, 'call the fisherman the Nellie-bird, but that is only another name for the beast, who I hope will never come to me.'

'To-day is Friday,' said Miss Pink, when she had put the plates away after their midday meal; 'and as it's Mrs. Pattimore's sewing-party, I'm sure that something will happen.'

'Yes,' said Miss Pink; 'it was on one of those days that I slipped down and hurt my nose. And on the other day, when Mr. Pattimore read a story called "The Modest Lovers," Mr. James Tarr came to the village and told us all about the horrible thing.'

Before she went out, Miss Pink peeped into the tiny office where Mr. Pink spent so much of his time.

'The estate accounts,' said Miss Pink, opening the door a very little, though enough for her small head, 'mustn't be interrupted.'

Mr. Pink was standing at his desk and writing. He looked as if the writing, or whatever it was he was at work upon, had carried him a very long way off from this base world.

'It's an agreement,' said Mr. Pink, hastily putting a large new sheet of blotting-paper over his work; 'it's the agreement between Mrs. Moggs and Mr. Roddy concerning the new lease upon her cottage. She is to have it for ever, if only—and I was just putting in the clause—she will consent to go down and look at the sea.'

'She will never do that,' said Miss Pink.

'Then we're all of us damned,' said the agent decidedly.

Miss Pink shivered. 'I hope that's not what's going to happen to-day,' she thought as she closed the door.

Miss Pink opened it again. 'If he comes,' she said, 'the front room's ready.'

'Yes, yes,' said Mr. Pink, 'I know.'

He did know, for this front room was Miss Pink's especial care. It was always dusted and the lamp trimmed and lit of an evening. Nothing was ever seen out of place in Miss Pink's front room. Even Mr. Caddy told his ducks about it all, and how Mr. Pink and she would sit in their kitchen upon a winter evening with only one candle burning, while the front room would be always lit up with a bright and well-trimmed lamp.

But only Miss Pink knew who was expected.

Mrs. Cheney and Mrs. Topple were already settled in chairs in the vicarage dining-room when Miss Pink was shown in by Rebecca Pring, who was herself to sit there soon as one of the party.

Mrs. Topple was already busy; she was embroidering, with green silk, clover leaves at each corner of a tablecloth. And the leaves were each four upon one stalk. Mrs. Topple didn't appear to take any notice of the other ladies who were in the room; and even when Miss Pink remarked to Mrs. Cheney that she believed something was going to happen, Mrs. Topple went on sewing and heeded nothing but her longed-for leaves.

Mrs. Cheney sat stoopingly, and pushed her needles into her knitting as if she pushed a fork into the ground. She looked very old, and replied to Miss Pink's remark by saying she hoped if anything happened that it wouldn't hurt her Simon.

Mary Gulliver and Dinah Pottle came in next. Mary's eyes were very wide open this afternoon, and she came in and sat down suddenly as though she were hunting the thimble and had seen it at once—upon the Dean's picture.

There were now angry sounds in the vicarage hall, as if two people were saying unpleasant things about one another, and Rebecca Pring thrust her mother into the room, hoping to prevent the words turning into blows.

Mrs. Pottle followed, very red in the face, as if she had been beating the ground again, and, muttering grimly that 'our clock don't never stop so long as 'tis wound,' she sat herself at a safe distance from her enemy.

Mrs. Pring was taken two ways by her thoughts: she wished to hate and she wished to look, because she carried with her in her head a very important mission from her husband.

Like so many more fathers, Mr. Pring believed nothing whatever that his daughter said; and so when she would come home and tell him how much the picture of the Dean knew about a girl's clothes and all other matters connected with young women, Mr. Pring would only remark that 'brother George of Dodder did use to say that no woon don't know nothing in Mockery.'

Mrs. Pring gazed at the Dean. She had heard and believed all that Rebecca said, and now it was her clear duty to convince her husband.

The Dean looked at her as a fine portrait of a man will usually do.

''E do say,' decided Mrs. Pring, committing her thoughts to memory, 'that wine and women be what 'e do know most about. 'E do know what a girl be like and a wine-bottle.'

Mrs. Pring blushed. The Dean stared at

her. 'Rebecca be right about 'e,' she whispered to the sewing in her lap; 'they eyes be everywhere.'

While Mrs. Pring was so wisely and truly deciding what the chief dignitaries of the Church are fondest of, Mrs. Pottle was looking at her with the same gleam in her eye as when she struck at the kittens, calling each one as she killed it 'Mrs. Pring.'

Mrs. Pottle hoped to see the lady of her hatred utterly shamed and naked. She noticed a tiny darn in the back of Mrs. Pring's blouse that wasn't well sewn. She fancied how nice it would be to get her nails into that place and to rip the whole garment down, and then all the ladies in the room could see Mrs. Pring's dirty under-bodice. ''T would show off she's manners to the public,' thought Mrs. Pottle.

But while watching Mrs. Pring, Mrs. Pottle noticed that she often looked at the large picture and smiled noddingly, as if she were inviting the man to change places with the sewing and to sit in her lap.

Mrs. Pottle now began to look at the Dean too. . . .

Mrs. Pattimore was reading *Martha's Choice* aloud, a work well chosen for the occasion, for it described how Martha preferred virginity and heaven, to hell and Mr. Robinson—a fine and noble gentleman who wore silk next to his skin and liked oysters.

Mrs. Pattimore always read in a sad, low tone, and when Martha bid her gentleman go—'anywhere, so long as she was left with her Bible'—she nearly cried, feeling, like Martha, that a book isn't a baby.

Mrs. Pattimore stopped reading, and looked up and sighed.

Miss Pink sighed too; she had fancied the Martha as herself, and she had been trying to blow her nose that was almost too small to find.

'I am afraid something is going to happen,' said Miss Pink.

Rebecca Pring looked at the Dean.

Sometimes in early summer an unexpected cloud rises out of a perfectly blue sky and darkens the land. A moment before the cloud comes all the land is still and shining. No wind ruffles the early corn, the sea glitters, and the green trees of Mockery wood are awake with beauty. And then all is changed: a creeping dimness arises out of nowhere and covers gloomily both the sea and the wood.

Mockery vicarage, as we have before hinted, was set a little higher than the rest of the village, so that from one of the dining-room windows the sea could be seen. But as it was always there, and was only the sea, very little notice was taken of it by the ladies who attended the work-party.

Miss Pink shivered; the dimness that had

overcast the sky could have no other meaning than that something was coming.

Miss Pink was sitting near to the window; she could see the Mockery bay, and the Blind Cow Rock.

The blind cow appeared more real in shadow than it had been a moment or two before in the sunshine. Miss Pink looked at the rock with fear. 'Suppose,' she thought, 'something jumped out of the sea and stood upon the rock—a nasty thing—what should she do?'

Whenever she was frightened, Miss Pink's usual plan was to hide under her large scarf that was so like a shawl and wait in patience with her tiny nose hidden until her fears left her. But she couldn't do so now, because her shawl was left upon one of Mrs. Pattimore's hall chairs.

And now, too, as though to add to the gloom of the day and to Miss Pink's fears, Mrs. Pattimore had stopped reading. No one spoke, either, for a silence had arrived that usually precedes a queer and unlooked-for event.

Even Mrs. Pottle, who as a rule took no notice of such subtle intimations of danger, felt a weight upon her that made her uneasy. And Mrs. Pring, who looked at the Dean, fancied that the eyes of the portrait rolled in its head, and its right hand moved threateningly.

And now, with the cloud above growing

darker than ever, the figure of a man—the new fisherman—opened the vicarage gate, exactly as any fisherman would do who had fish to sell, and entered the gravel drive.

The fisherman appeared very much the same in looks as when Mrs. Pattimore had seen him drifting in his boat in the bay. He now wore a cap, and showed as he walked the light step, the unhesitating manner, of a young man who knows what he is doing.

Mary Gulliver, who had felt in no small measure the queer silence, had looked as soon as the gate had clicked to see who it was, expecting, perhaps, to behold one of those horrid monsters that according to her father's map inhabited the known world.

'Oh, it's only the fisherman,' gasped Mary, trying to allay by this simple disclosure of who had really come the strange and uneasy feeling that pervaded the room. But the ominous sense of something odd wasn't to be driven off so easily, for the presence of the fine tall and bearded figure, though clad in the usual fisherman's jersey, and going past the window to the back door with a basket of mackerel in his hand, had already become an important figure at the meeting, and intended to stay there very unforgettably.

As the fisherman passed the window, a clap of thunder that appeared never to end—continued to reverberate around the Mockery hills for some seconds—made Miss Pink start so violently that her ball of wool (for she was knitting) rolled all along the room and hid itself at last under Mrs. Pring's skirts.

And then the knock came at the back door.

Nothing in this world can so terrify a group of simple people, each more nervous than the other, than a knock at the back door.

It may be, and I daresay that this is the case, that we fancy that any knock, even though we think we know who the knocker really is, may be the post that we all wot of, that is to call us hence once and for ever.

The fisherman knocked again. The silence in the vicarage dining-room was more intense than ever, though each lady thought—and even Mrs. Pring and Mrs. Pottle forgot to hate one another in consideration of such an exciting situation—that something ought to be done.

For no one, the ladies rightly felt—no, not even a seller of things, and those things fishes—should be allowed to remain knocking at the back door without any notice being taken of his being there.

Rebecca had once mildly risen and looked at her mistress, who however gave her no command, and so the girl sat down.

As well as the servant, each one in the room —and even Mrs. Topple had raised her head from her flowers—had looked at Mrs. Pattimore when the fisherman went by the window.

Mrs. Pattimore blushed as scarlet as if some one had set a match to her, but she made no motion and said no word as to what should be done. The first knock had been a gentle one, but each one of the company expected, having her own experience at back doors to go by—and even Mrs. Pattimore had been forced round to the Cheneys' back door more than once—that the second would be louder.

And so it was; and then the third came—not angrily, but merely such a knocking as implied the natural desire of the knocker to be attended to.

To relieve her suspense as to what would happen, Rebecca looked hard at the Dean; 'Would he,' she wondered—he looked so life-like—'step out of the frame and kindly go to open the door?' But as he didn't—and Rebecca explained that by merely saying to herself, "Tain't no girl who be knocking'—she couldn't help wishing that Mrs. Moggs had allowed herself to leave her shop to attend the sewing meeting.

'Mrs. Moggs would 'ave seen to 'e,' thought Rebecca.

A moment later, when the dining-room door opened, Miss Pink drew up her legs, and tried at the same moment to hide her nose and herself with her knitting, believing that the horned beast had leaped from the Blind Cow Rock to the vicarage dining-room in one bound.

'It's only Mr. Pattimore,' said Mary Gulliver.

And so it was, for Mr. Pattimore, who was busy in his attic about his next Sunday's sermon, having removed himself from the dining-room when the visitors arrived, had been disturbed by the knocking. He now said, though a little pettishly for so chaste a man: 'How can I work at this text, Dorcas— "I say again, Let no man think me a fool"— while all this loud knocking goes on at the back door?'

Rebecca rose from her seat, but Mrs. Pattimore, who trembled now as well as blushed, stopped her going out.

'I think I had better go,' she said.

Mr. Pattimore had already begun to climb the stairs to his attic; he hadn't dared to look at his wife.

'For the mackerel may not be fresh enough for my husband, and if they aren't fresh it would be better for him to be as though he had none.' In her extreme nervousness Mrs. Pattimore had caught at another of his favourite texts.

She went out and softly shut the door after her. Mrs. Cheney, bent and withered, was the sort of woman who never has much to say, all her affairs being so wrapped up in the fine young god that she worshipped—her son Simon. When it thundered, she feared that her Simon might be harmed by it, or at least get a wetting, with no young woman to shield him, for Mrs. Cheney had an entire mother's belief that everything in the world should be sacrificed in the cause of her wonderful boy. Mrs. Cheney now began to explain how very important a matter it was, buying fish at the back door, and that when she bought them for Simon—she had no need to mention Mr. Cheney, who was but another worker in the cause of the pretty god—she always took them into her hands to see if the shining, slippery things were as stiff as they should be. And if like that—and Mrs. Cheney nodded as if she were telling Simon to be careful about the bones—they must have been caught, as the fishermen always say they are, in the early hours of the morning. Or if limp and dull-coloured, they would have been purchased at Weyminster and merely carried to Mockery to sell again.

'Simon won't touch nothing that bain't the best,' she said, looking at the other Mary; whose turn it was, now that Mrs. Pattimore was gone, to blush.

Having said this, and feeling that she had said enough, Mrs. Cheney looked at Miss Pink, who had somewhat recovered from her fright and was knitting again.

Mrs. Pottle and Mrs. Pring were listening; each had forgotten the other. They were listening as folk will who want to catch—

though they know this to be impossible—a distant word.

All waited, and the Dean, at whom each looked in turn, seemed to wait too.

Something was going on at the back door, and even Dinah, though she felt that a wood was the better place for hidden doings, wished she was there to see.

Every one listened, as though it were a matter of life and death to them to know whether the fine mackerel, fresh caught as they really were, were three for sixpence or four for ninepence.

It was Mary Gulliver, and as a child she had played the game, 'Who speaks first becomes the sow'—and she always was—who now broke the silence by saying with a gasp, 'What do 'ee think Mrs. Pattimore be a-doing wi' thik fisherman?'

To aid herself in giving a right answer to this question Miss Pink looked out of the window.

The vicarage gate, that had up to that moment been as silent as any gate that behaves properly should be, now showed an unusual liveliness, for seated upon it, in a way that wasn't exactly modest, was Esther, the naughtiest child in Mockery. And as though to give all possible support to their leader, the rest of the wolfish pack, with hands through the bars, were demanding with shouts and clamour that the Nellie-bird should be given up to them.

''E be a-gone thik way,' cried Esther, pointing to the path that led round the house to the back door.

'Send 'e out for we to throw mud at,' called out the others. All the children now set up a loud howling and demanded with many threats that the Nellie-bird should be let out of the gate.

Even the Dean had few eyes now left to look at him, for the window demanded all, and before Mary Gulliver had time to gasp out, ''Tis 'e wi' they fishes,' the fisherman passed the window again, but not alone. Mrs. Pattimore was with him.

The fisherman walked beside her.

The children cried out the louder.

The cloud that had made all things so dim that afternoon now broke as if in two halves. And the sun poured down hot and loving.

The fisherman had taken off his cap, perhaps when the lady first opened the door to him, and hadn't troubled to put it on again, and he now carried it in his hand. He was talking pleasantly to Mrs. Pattimore, who, though she hardly answered at all, looked up at him with a blissful devotion.

'The Nellie-bird, the Nellie-bird!' shouted the children.

Mrs. Pattimore stood uncertain while the

fisherman opened the gate; she felt that she ought to try to prevent the children from hurting this newcomer who was being made a mock of; and yet by the look of him he appeared to be well able to take care of himself.

He waved her back, and before little Esther could quite decide what he was doing to her he had filled her apron with fishes.

While Esther divided the spoil, which she did very fairly, the fisherman strode boldly across the fields and towards the sea.

Mrs. Pattimore entered the dining-room, but instead of looking in a dreary way at the Dean, as she would sometimes do, she looked with a happy smile at Miss Pink, and taking her almost into her arms she kissed her three times.

Chapter 14

MR. PRING TALKS TO THE STONES

MR. JAMES PRING always spoke to the weather; he considered that the weather was a person that could be addressed as either 'he' or 'she.' ''E be bad-tempered to-day,' James would say to his wife, if there chanced to be rain-clouds abroad. Or else when the wind blew, 'She don't care whose thatch she do blow off, she bain't particular.'

When Mr. Pring named the weather as 'she,' Mrs. Pring often misunderstood him, and fancied that he referred to Mrs. Pottle.

'She bain't worth a cow's tail, thik 'oman,' said Mrs. Pring one fine hot morning when she observed her husband to stare hard at the sky.

Mr. Pring looked from the sky to the Mockery cliff, beyond which lay the villages of Dodder, Madder, Norbury, and all the rest of the world.

'Thik picture,' remarked Mr. Pring, look-ing from the Mockery cliff and at his wife, 'that did step out of 'is frame to kiss Miss Pink at party, do know of a letter.'

Mrs. Pring looked at her husband with pride; he was famed as a messenger. This fame had arisen in a very simple manner, because Mr. Pring had always taken the trouble to inform the good folk of Mockery, whenever he met any of them, that he had never lost a letter.

In the ever-green valley of Mockery Gap only the stranger oddities of men and women outlive their lives. Riches pass there and are gone; goodness and charity, poverty—too common, perhaps, to be mentioned—go too; but a man who has once been credited with eating a dozen eggs for his dinner lives for ever. And so with Mr. Pring; for he with his fame—though only one person, and she a lady, had ever entrusted him with a letter—will most likely be handed down as the faithful deliverer of all the private and unposted correspondence through all time.

The letter from which Mr. Pring's fame had arisen—for from its presence in his trousers pocket he had acclaimed himself to the world as 'the one to carry a message'—the letter (and the time has come for us to discover it) had been handed to Mr. Pring by Miss Pink, then a girl, one autumn day when the mist hung low in the lane that led to the sea. Fifteen years have gone by since love had set Miss Pink's heart a-dancing, a heart that must have been as large as her nose was small. Mr. Pink had only just been set up at his desk, with Mr. Roddy's affairs all about him to attend to, and he had visited the shop but a few times, and Mrs. Moggs had hardly rung her bells to him, nor given him the exciting hopes for her eternal salvation, when the letter was written.

It was February and leap year, and the last day of the month too, and Miss Pink had gone out, because the sun was pleasantly warm, to walk in the fields. Miss Pink had been looking for water-cress, a weed that her brother was extremely fond of; and after taking out of the ditch as much as she chose, she chanced to look up and saw Mr. Gulliver, who had been a widower for a year, playing with the rabbits. Mr. Gulliver wasn't alone, for his daughter Mary was with him, and she was stroking a tiny rabbit that appeared to have entirely lost its natural timidity.

Near by upon the grass there were snares that were never set, a gun that was never fired, and nets that were never used.

Mr. Gulliver, being a rather oddly-made portion of Mockery clay, had discovered that rabbits were fine things for Mary to play with, though rather dull to eat.

And from that day Miss Pink loved Mr. Gulliver.

That same evening Mr. Pink said to his sister, 'I cannot find, dear, any mention in my accounts of Mr. Gulliver's rent-day.'

'Perhaps it's the 29th of February—that may be his day for payment,' replied Miss Pink.

'Oh, very likely,' said Mr. Pink.

Miss Pink wrote her letter.

Dear Mr. Gulliver,—I hope you aren't troubled about my picking your water-cress in the meadow. I have never seen any rabbits eating it, and they might drown themselves if they tried to.

I have never thought of any one before, but I love you because you let Mary play with the rabbits. I have noticed in church that there is a tear in the back of the child's little coat; if you will let me marry you I will mend it.—I remain, yours devotedly,

Martha Pink.

Being such a timid person, one can easily imagine that Miss Pink hardly felt brave enough to deliver this letter with her own hands, and so she gave it to Mr. Pring, who promised to deliver it that very afternoon.

But Mr. Pring had only taken the letter out of his pocket some half-dozen times in half an hour when he began to feel that fame was come upon him.

'Postman do think fine of 'eself,' he said to the spade that he carried, walking to his home instead of to Mr. Gulliver's; 'but he bain't nothing so careful as Pring.'

After many days of waiting for her answer, Miss Pink decided that Mr. Gulliver had dropped the letter in the field and that the rabbits had eaten it. And she began to think that she couldn't love rabbits as well as she used to. Sometimes, when she thought no one was listening, and she saw the rabbits in Mr. Gulliver's field, she would say to them unhappily, 'You shouldn't have eaten my letter up—you naughty rabbits!'

But was it the rabbits? Miss Pink thought as she grew older that it might have been the horned beast from the sea. Perhaps he had pounced out upon poor Pring and torn the letter from him and then gone down to the sea again.

'The sea is very dangerous,' Miss Pink said to her brother, when she decided that the beast might have done it.

'No, it's very beautiful,' said Mr. Pink. . . .

Mr. Pring held up his spade and pointed to the skies; he wished to show his wife that the skies and the weather were one and the same.

'They wide skies,' said Mr. Pring, 'be against I; for whenever I be minded to climb to top of cliff and to pull loose stones out of road, for fear Mr. Hunt, who be worse than all they damned surveyors, mid come by, 'e do come.'

'Who do come?' asked Mrs. Pring.

'Rain,' replied her husband dolefully. "E do come; and even when I do take an' crack stones in lane, wi' me back turned, she do blow upon me from behind.'

Mr. Pring began to move slowly; he had decided that, whatever the weather did, it was his duty to try to remove from the cliff road the stones that Mr. Hunt complained about. No one ever left his home, though for only a few hours and upon the smallest and most necessary occasion, with graver foreboding than did Mr. Pring. He always supposed that when he went off to the roads, Mrs. Pottle—and Mrs. Pring always said that she could do it—would change herself into a nasty dog, and bite his lame cow or else torment the little pigs.

Mr. Pring, as well as Mary Gulliver, felt the nakedness of the outside world, where one might walk in solitude for a mile and see no one.

The more ordinary and simple-minded a person is, the less able is he to enjoy solitude; and any word from man or woman, be that word ever so plain, is far more acceptable to such a one than the choicest gusts of wind from heaven.

Mr. Pring never approached anything that wasn't a tree or a hill, but that had a more human look, without the greatest inquisitiveness.

He appeared now to be more than usually hopeful of meeting some one to talk to, because since the arrival of those fine visitors upon the cliff Mockery Gap had plenty to say for itself.

Pring was full of news, that bubbled as he walked and sometimes broke out of him in a groan of suppressed interest and sometimes in a chuckle.

As soon as he had entered the lane that led to the cliff, something had attracted his notice that wasn't the mere dullness of empty nature, but rather belonged, and excitedly belonged, to the human.

To any one who knows a scene very well, the presence of something stationary, where nothing of the kind is likely to stand, at once arouses an interest and calls for further investigation.

The object that Mr. Pring saw looked black in the white cliff road, and was set half-way up the hill, looking in Mr. Pring's eyes like one of the monsters that Mr. Gulliver talked so much about.

Mr. Pring hadn't walked far before he decided that the monster in question was nothing more terrible than Mr. Hunt's motor car, that had evidently broken down going up the steep place in the hill. Mr. Pring quickened his pace, for before him was no dead nature, or even a surprising monster, but a mere human accident, and so a kindly amusement for Mr. Pring.

When Mr. Pring reached the car, he perceived that there were two gentlemen in the road instead of one, as he had at first supposed, one of whom was addressing the other, who heard his words a little impatiently.

'You ought to be kinder to poor Mrs. Moggs,' Mr. Pink, the second of the two gentlemen, was mildly saying. 'You ought to be kinder, Mr. Hunt, for it's not at all proper in a Christian country to shout and tell a soul that one day may be saved—and so may be above us all—that she's only a stupid old woman.'

Mr. Hunt, although Squire Roddy and Mr. James Tarr always spoke well of him, and praised his strong-minded Conservatism, wasn't the politest of men to all comers, and he considered that moment a suitable one for saying that he hadn't stopped in the road to listen to any damned sermon.

'I know my duties,' he shouted, 'and I don't require to be taught by Roddy's dependants.'

Mr. Pink bowed. 'He hoped,' he said, 'he had done no harm in speaking a word for Mrs. Moggs, but he knew she felt unkind things, and perhaps might if she heard too many of them be prevented from viewing the loveliness of the blue sea.'

Mr. Hunt, being a fine imitator of great men, now shook his fist, because he had once seen Mr. Tarr shake his fist at his old gardener, Mr. Dobbin.

Mr. Hunt shook his fist first at Mr. Pink

and then at the car. After which he applied himself to the latter with such anger, that with Pring pushing behind—and even Mr. Pink out of the kindness of his heart lent a willing hand—the machine started going and was in a moment gone, leaving Mr. Pring looking at the loose stones in the road that had caused the trouble, and Mr. Pink looking at nature and evidently wishing to forget man.

Mr. Pring was the first to break the silence of the hill, by addressing a remark to the stones in the road.

'They grand gentlemen,' remarked Mr. Pring, looking down, 'do like to excite themselves.'

Mr. Pring looked up at his companion and winked; but seeing no response in Mr. Pink, who was leaning forward watching intently a moving figure in the fields of Dodder, Mr. Pring addressed himself to the stones again, that appeared to be the most interested listeners.

'Mockery Gap,' said Mr. Pring, sitting down by the roadside so as to be nearer to his listeners, 'be the place for happenings. Simon Cheney do make things happen to maidens, that Parson Pattimore do name sinning in 's sermons. 'Tis true,' said Mr. Pring, kicking a stone to make it listen the better, 'that Caddy do tell his ducks about what women do want, and that poor Mrs. Pattimore do lie in a wide bed and cry at night-time. 'Tis nice to live in Mockery, where Mrs. Moggs do ring she's happy bells, and schoolmistress do search all the fields over for a leaf to cure all afflictions. 'Tis nice to hear Mrs. Pottle cry out in lane, "Damn and blast all they Prings!" 'Tis nice to hear she talk. 'Tis nice to hear wold Gulliver tell t' other Mary about savage demons and devils.'

Mr. Pring took up three stones out of the road and placed them upon the bank, so that they might be out of the way of Mr. Hunt's car when he came another day to visit Mrs. Moggs.

Mr. Pink gave no heed to Mr. Pring's talk; he overlooked Mockery sadly, as if he fancied the conversion of Mrs. Moggs to be an event very far off, and very much hindered too by the visits of Mr. Hunt. Above Mr. Pink the sky had grown darker, a circumstance that caused Pring to grow suspicious, and to wonder who it was that the agent was watching for. Mr. Pring always fancied that any changed behaviour of the weather was owing to the weather's love or anger to him or else to another.

And so, seeing that Mr. Pink was watching some one, he fancied that it must be that some one who had caused the displeasure in the skies and brought up the dark cloud. Being familiar with the habits and manners of Mr. Pink, and regarding himself as almost one of

the family because Miss Pink had once entrusted him with a letter, Mr. Pring, raising
himself, demanded a little pertly, 'Who be
thee out watching for, Agent?'

'The fisherman,' said Mr. Pink quietly.

Mr. Pring looked up at the cloud, as if he
fancied the fisherman might come out from it.

''Ave 'ee spoken to thik Nellie-bird?' he
inquired.

'The fisherman wished to meet me here,'
said Mr. Pink.

Sometimes when one has watched for some
while upon a country hill for an expected
comer, the object of our watch seems to appear
as though by magic, and stands beside us—
perhaps arriving from a direction that we least
expect—in a moment, when we fancy that he
or she may yet be far away.

The sudden arrival of the fisherman, who
now stood in the road beside Mr. Pink, created
such an unlooked-for disturbance in Mr.
Pring's mind, that had the cloud changed
into the form of Mrs. Pottle—Mr. Pottle
never counted as anything in the world—and
begun beating him with lightning flashes,
the road-mender wouldn't have shown more
surprise.

Mr. Pring looked fearfully at Mr. Pink,
who, standing beside the fisherman, appeared
to have become a different person.

The usual air of dejected humility that

Mr. Pink carried with him was changed to a strength of manner and look that made Mr. Pring stare and stare again. And the agent's face, usually so sallow, shone now with a strange beauty, lit up by a sudden sunbeam.

It was only a moment before that Pring had noticed the cloud, and now here was the sun shining full upon Mr. Pink and the fisherman!

Mr. Pring, who disliked the thought of art magic, was willing enough to account for the sudden change in Mr. Pink's look by the natural fact that the sun had broken through the darkness of the cloud and shone upon the cliff side.

And when Mr. Pink sat down upon the grass with the fisherman beside him, Pring was the first to speak, for he considered himself as good as they, and wished to show it.

''Tis thik fisherman,' he remarked reassuringly, 'that they children do shout after.'

The fact that the children could shout after him strengthened at once—as he mentioned it —Mr. Pring's opinion of himself and properly lowered the fisherman.

'The Nellie-bird, they do call 'ee. And thee be come from they islands, bain't 'ee? and islands be t' other side of sea?'

The fisherman nodded.

'Mrs. Pottle,' said Pring, who, after the manner of all people the world over, liked to get in the first blow at an enemy—'Mrs. Pottle do walk about telling folk that in they islands thee 've left three maidens in trouble.'

The fisherman laughed lightly and happily.

Mr. Pring hadn't expected a laugh at all, but had counted upon a sour look from the fisherman directed against the absent lady.

If the laugh took Mr. Pring by surprise, it certainly had the same effect upon the dark cloud, through which the sunbeam had broken, for the cloud now entirely disappeared and the heavens were blue. Mr. Pring looked up distrustfully, wondering perhaps whether 'she,' the weather, was in any way related to the new fisherman that the bad children of Mockery called after. The sun had shone out more readily than usual when so heavy a cloud was in the heavens.

John Pring felt uneasy.

But then here was the fisherman sitting upon the bank beside Mr. Pink who was as common in Mockery as any gatepost that is seen each day.

Mr. Pring now felt that he must do a further honour to the village convention—scandal. 'Mr. Caddy were telling 'is ducks a story yesterday,' said Mr. Pring, addressing himself again to the stones. 'And they wise ducks do swim about pond, though they be runners, and quack when 'e do talk.

'Mr. Caddy were telling the ducks how the new fisherman, who bain't got no name only

Nellie-bird, did spy Esther Pottle lying out amongst the bluebells in meadow.'

Mr. Pring hesitated and shook his head sadly; evidently the idea of Esther lying in that way troubled him, for he continued dolefully: 'The sun were burning down upon she, and there the maiden did lie— an' mother at home do say she don't dress proper—and did hide she's face all in they blue flowers. No, no, 'twasn't Simon that did find her laid out; 'twas 'e, so 'tis said.'

Mr. Pring nodded at the fisherman, who rested happily beside Mr. Pink upon the warm bank.

'Esther and I were happy,' said the fisherman.

Mr. Pring hadn't expected a remark that so confessed to everything, and so he returned dolefully to the ducks again.

'Kissing be only a little thing to a girl, Caddy did say to the runners, an' maiden were lying out straight and laughing amongst the bluebells, but when Mr. Pattimore came into field Esther did cry out and run off. An' she be a bad woon, though 'twere only kisses thik day that ducks do know of.'

Mr. Pring had told his story to the stones, and had not looked up while he was telling it. And now that he looked up to see what effect his recital of the facts had upon the chief actor, he was surprised and a little crestfallen too to perceive that the female wanton of his story, the naughty Esther herself, was listening. And not listening alone, but lying out in her usual happy and free fashion, as though pink flesh was more pretty than clothes, beside the fisherman, with her moist hand in his.

But odd happenings have a way of continuing chapter after chapter when once the preface is over, and now like wolfish dogs the whole pack of the Mockery children burst upon the simple group upon the hillside, calling out the sort of noisy things that are usually said when any one leaves the herd to seek a lover in the wilderness.

The fisherman, upon whose account and Esther's all the clamour was raised, now stood up; and he still holding the girl's hand, while Mr. Pink, being invited to follow, walked upon the other side, the three went slowly down the hill, followed by the children, who made the most of their usual cry of derision—'The Nellie-bird!'

Mr. Pring being left alone, began slowly to shovel up the loose stones, which he placed in little heaps by the side of the road.

After doing so, the roadman leant against a post that in distant times had held up a rail, and looked down to and over the village of Mockery. When so many strange things were happening that hadn't in the least to do with him, Mr. Pring began thoughtfully to doubt his own importance in a place where scandal as soon as mentioned now became reality.

He slowly took out of his pocket the letter that Miss Pink had given him. He had carried the letter for fifteen years, for whenever he looked at it he always felt his importance as a messenger. He spelt the name, 'Mr. Gulliver,' and put the letter back into his pocket.

'I bain't nothing,' said Mr. Pring, and looked grimly at the village below him; 'for I be better than postman.'

The sun shone graciously with its true summer heat, swifts flashed by with a hiss of wings, blue butterflies toyed wantonly, and little brown spiders crept amongst the warmed grass. Mr. Pring looked at all this and expressed in words his own ideas. ''Tis a pity thik fisherman don't drown 'isself,' he said.

Chapter 15

THE FISHERMAN WILL NOT
BE ROUSED

ALL things that happened at Mockery contributed to the fierce flame of anger that burnt up the hearts of the Prings and the Pottles. Even when Mr. Pring let his cap fall into a grave that he was digging, and had no mind to dig it out again, his complaints about the loss were overheard by Mrs. Pottle and raised a storm.

'Folks,' called out Mrs. Pottle from over the hedge, 'mid be allowed to bury anything these days; and to think that poor Cousin Hilda should be seen wearing thik dirty cap of Pring's on Judgment Day, dying as she did out at service; 'twill damn the poor maid to be seen in en.'

Mrs. Pring came out to the fray.

''Twould be well,' she shouted,' if thee's Hilda did wear a man's cap on last day, for they wise elders and beasts who do stare so mid fancy that she did 'ave woon husband, instead of a dozen chaps after her, although it wasn't a cap that she did fancy the most.'

'What were it then,' hissed Mrs. Pottle, 'that poor Hilda did fancy?'

'Sunday trousers,' replied Mrs. Pring quietly.

Though she held no sword in her hand,

Mrs. Pottle had an egg that she had just taken out of a nest under the hedge. She threw the egg at Mrs. Pring.

The egg burst upon the cottage wall.

Mrs. Pring went indoors laughing.

Mrs. Pottle went in too to look at her clock. This clock had always entered into the grand quarrel as one of the best known and most used of Mrs. Pottle's household gods. It ranked in its possessor's eyes as something that stood in the front rank to withstand any attempt that the Prings might make to boast of their pigs or their lame cow.

The clock had suffered in one of the enemy's charges, for once when Mrs. Pottle was in the back garden, and unthinkingly left the door open, Mrs. Pring had taken this chance to throw a stone, with so good an aim that it broke the face of the clock and knocked out the hour hand.

But this treatment, that gave to the clock a kind of martyr's crown, and also left with it a daily doubt as to what the hour was, made it appear even more valuable and important in the eyes of its owners.

When Mrs. Pring put a large padlock upon the garden well that Mrs. Pottle used to dip in for water by the right of custom, Mrs. Pottle looked at the spoilt face of her clock for advice. She had to wash clothes to-day, and the nearest water was Mr. Caddy's pond.

Whenever Mrs. Pottle went forth upon any errand there was always a chance that she might meet some one whom she could turn by a wise word or two into as fierce an enemy of the Prings as she herself was.

Beside the pond, lying idly with his feet in the sun and his head shaded, was the new fisherman. He lay upon the soft moss and clover in indulgent ease, looking now at Mr. Caddy's ducks and now upwards through the sweetest and most delightful of rich green leaves. Mrs. Pottle had never spoken to the fisherman before; at least she had never gone beyond the usual conversation of a lady who wishes to buy something as cheaply as she can, and knows meanwhile that she is being listened to by her neighbour. She was away from home now and she could say what she chose. Although Mrs. Pottle had always blamed the fisherman for idling away his time instead of going off in his boat, and also for selling what fish he did catch so cheaply to the Prings, she now hoped to enlist him upon her side. To do this, she knew that the first thing was to obtain a proper respect towards herself from the fisherman, for no one in Mockery ever fought upon a losing side if he could help it.

"'Tain't every one who do know the right time of day,' she said impressively. 'An' a good clock, though 'tis me own'—Mrs. Pottle looked down modestly—'be worth some money.'

The fisherman smiled at the ducks.

Mrs. Pottle had evidently impressed him; she thought it now proper, according to the usual Mockery convention, to take another line to compliment him.

''Tisn't every one,' she said with a little cough, 'who do rush and go, here now and there now, always a-doing, who be the hardest worker.'

Mrs. Pottle filled her bucket, set it down in the lane, and looked at Mr. Caddy's ducks.

The fisherman moved lazily; he was evidently enjoying a time of entire contentment and rest. He seemed pleased to see Mrs. Pottle there, and pleased to see the ducks.

''Tis nice to think,' said Mrs. Pottle, 'that green grass be useful to some folk, and no doubt God did mean thik to be laid upon. 'Twas a pity that poor Mr. Dobbin didn't use 'imself to such holy comforts, for what sense were it for 'e to go a-fishing and all to give away a crab to they Prings?'

Mrs. Pottle leant over her bucket and touched the handle; in this posture she still continued to talk. 'Mrs. Pring be the woon to insult folk who be givers, and she do hate a fisherman, and there be some one that she do tell of called the Nellie-bird, who she do say 'ave a-got only one jersey to wear both weekdays and Sundays. A good clock be better than a lame cow.'

The fisherman, though not roused to words, appeared to be listening.

Mrs. Pottle raised her bucket and stood with it in her hand.

'Mrs. Pring do often talk of Dobbin,' she said, with a gesture as if she threw her thoughts back to times gone by. She turned sharply to the fisherman: 'But Pring do say that poor Dobbin weren't nothing such a lazy, lousy beggar as thee be.'

The fisherman lay silent; he slept.

In a few moments Mrs. Pottle was back again in her garden.

Mrs. Pring was turning the key in the new padlock upon the well cover; she had just been drawing water.

'One of thee's friends,' Mrs. Pottle shouted, 'who do give away 'is stinking fish to 'ee, be waiting to cuddle thee's maid down by Caddy's pond, and what be she to cuddle but only a servant?'

Mrs. Pring pointed pleasantly to the road that was but a few yards away.

The fisherman was walking by, as one who is idle walks upon a warm summer's day. He was smiling.

Chapter 16

THE WHITE MICE

PEOPLE, although they may believe in God, often think very differently about Him. Mr. Pattimore believed in His Name, which Name he surrounded with attributes as cold as ice. In his own attic bed that resembled God's Name in its coldness he hoped to harden himself and become fit to be a dean, though so far in his life he had not even had a call to become a canon.

Mr. Gulliver didn't take God in the least as Mr. Pattimore took Him, but rather fancied Him as a humorous gentleman, a little like Mr. James Tarr, and able, indeed willing, to supply the world with a good store of monsters and to bring the Nellie-bird to Mockery Gap as a stray fisherman.

If Mrs. Topple had been asked where she supposed God might be found, she would have replied that when she had once found the clover with four leaves God would be standing near by in the shape of an all-wise doctor.

Mr. Pink saw God as a vast sea of ever-changing colour, a sea that is beyond human vision, though the blessed may pass over there to a country that is very fair and is called Eternity....

Mr. Pink was at work at his desk, and the

summer sun, as inquisitive as great people always are, peeped in upon him.

Mr. Pink had been asked in a letter to try to discover—'It's Miss Ogle who thought something ought to be done,' Mr. Roddy had said—the arrears of rent that Mr. Gulliver owed to the Roddy estate.

He was now trying to decide a point that interested him more than the additional sum: that was, how much he ought to take off from the bill, because Gulliver had made at his own expense a new gate for Mr. Caddy's cottage that went with the farm.

He was upon the point of taking away £1, 15s. 6d., the supposed value of the gate that Mr. Caddy liked so much to lean upon when he talked to the ducks, from Mr. Gulliver's debt of £789, 14s. 3½d., when Miss Pink put her head into the door and said that a basket had been left by the fisherman for Mrs. Moggs, that he wished Mr. Pink to give to her.

'I believe they 're white mice,' said Miss Pink, who had, it must be owned, peeped in to see.

Mr. Pink closed his ledger. He decided as the heavy book shut that he had better pay to Mr. Gulliver the £1, 15s. 6d. that the estate owed him, which would save the trouble of an extra sum.

Mr. Pink peeped at the mice too.

'Mr. James Tarr said they would save her life and prevent her being lonely,' he said, looking with admiration at the mice.

'Will you take them to her now?' asked Miss Pink, lifting one of the mice up in her hand and kissing it.

'Perhaps I had better,' replied Mr. Pink.

Miss Pink looked out of the door and watched him go. She stood upon the door-step wrapped in her shawl, and she hoped, as she always did when she watched him go even to the nearest cottage to look at some repairs being done, that nothing would happen to him.

When Mr. Pink turned the corner to go to the shop, Miss Pink turned her eyes to the sea.

The sun—for the summer of our story was an unusually fine one—shone above in all happiness, and the only doleful object that Miss Pink could see to remind her of her fears was the Blind Cow Rock, that looked a dead black.

Miss Pink entered the house again and began to dust the front room.

Although it was summer, she filled the lamp with oil and trimmed the wick, and then, standing beside the table, Miss Pink looked at the front-room chair and began to wonder about the visitor she expected.

It wasn't Mr. Gulliver now; her letter must have been given to him; Mr. Pring the good messenger could never have taken fifteen years to deliver it.

She had thought certainly that he would have come, and she would have found him, bowed in by Mr. Pink—for no man in the world was so gentle and polite as her brother—and sitting in that best chair! The white mice had reminded her—of course he would have brought her a tiny baby rabbit for a gift.

But now what was Miss Pink thinking of, and whom was she expecting as she looked at the plush-covered chair?

She had never told her brother, but still she had told herself that she didn't want to go.

'I don't want to go,' said Miss Pink, her tiny nose almost disappearing into her shawl; 'I don't want to go, because I love my dear brother, and I don't like the rude way the sexton shovels the rough earth down upon one. I know it must hurt, and besides for a long time I have known, ever since my pain began, that the horrid beast that Mr. Tarr told us about—is death.'

Miss Pink straightened the sofa cushion, she dusted the window and looked out.

The black rock was there. . . .

Mr. Pink carried the basket carefully, for although the mice were covered with a cloth he feared that they might escape, and every now and again he peeped in to see if they were safe.

Mrs. Moggs was standing behind her counter when Mr. Pink entered her shop. She was telling Esther Pottle, who for some unexplained reason had now learned to stand quiet and good, about all the rude things that the postmaster had said to her; and Esther looked at her, hoping all the time that Mrs. Moggs talked that the bells would begin to ring.

Mr. Pink sighed as he placed the basket upon the counter, because he had almost wished as he stepped along the stone path in the sun that the mice were for him.

'The fisherman——'

'You mean the Nellie-bird, Mr. Pink,' said Esther.

Mr. Pink nodded. 'The fisherman thought you would like to play with them when you feel lonely, though they 're nowhere near as beautiful as the sea.'

'I'm sure the sea 's nothing like so pretty,' replied Mrs. Moggs, nodding and ringing both her bells at the same moment. 'I'll let them sleep here'—Mrs. Moggs opened a drawer— 'and they can't hurt the postal orders, because they 're all in the next one.'

Mr. Pink leaned over the counter. 'The sea 's still there,' he whispered, 'and I beg you to go down to it. I believe you could pray there better than in any church you know. There is some one who isn't well, Mrs. Moggs, that I want you to pray for.'

Mrs. Moggs looked at Mr. Pink and her bells hung silent.

'I know,' she said.

'You will come one day?'

'Yes, one day,' Mrs. Moggs replied. . . .

Mr. Pink had turned to wave his hand, as he used to do whenever he went two hundred yards away from her, when he left his sister standing upon their cottage steps. But he couldn't return at that moment to see the difference. The difference, that he always noticed now when he came in to her, the growing look of fear in her eyes, as though something hidden was dragging her, hour by hour and day by day, nearer and yet nearer to the dreadful darkness.

'Perhaps the sea might help, or the fisherman. I can't bear to see her in pain,' said Mr. Pink.

Mr. Pink walked down the lane and stepped upon the soft warm grass of the meadow that led to the sea.

Mockery was out to play that afternoon; cries came to him from the children, who were chasing Esther and calling after her rude country words about the Nellie-bird being her lover.

Mrs. Topple was wandering in the fields, and looking sadly about her because she had been so long wandering and had found nothing.

Dinah Pottle was lying in the wood upon the very moss-covered stump where the hermit of old used to pray, hoping Simon would come; but God Simon was upon the hill with the other Mary, while Rebecca watched them from the vicarage window.

Mrs. Pattimore was dusting the Dean.

Caddy was telling his ducks a new story; and Mr. Gulliver was remarking to the hay as he turned it over—for perhaps he had looked up to the hill as well as Rebecca—that if anything ever happened to his daughter Mary while she was yet unwedded, he would renounce her for ever and cast her out from his home.

Standing upon those yellow sands, Mr. Pink wished that he had been able to persuade Mrs. Moggs to come and look at the sea.

The sea was so still and clear, that Mr. Pink could notice the little fish that were swimmimg in it, and even the coloured shining stones that were at the bottom.

'If only she would come,' said Mr. Pink, 'I feel sure that her soul would leap and cry out for eternity.'

He looked further away, to where the sea and the sky met one another.

'Her soul would not stay as far as her eyes can see, but it would rush on until the glory of God is reached.'

Mr. Pink hadn't noticed it before, but he now saw that a boat was sailing by. Hardly sailing, perhaps, because there was almost a dead calm, but leisurely gliding, and appearing as if it were a part of the summer sky and the sea.

The fisherman was asleep in the stern. Mr. Pink had come there on purpose to ask the fisherman about his sister; he must know of something, he felt sure—some seaweed, perhaps—that would ease the continuous pain that she suffered. Mr. Pink called, but the fisherman didn't awake.

'The new fisherman is wonderful,' said Mr. Pink. 'Esther, who used to be so rude, is a good girl now because she loves him; he found those white mice for Mrs. Moggs; and even Mrs. Pattimore begins to sing in her garden; and one day he will show Mrs. Topple where the precious clover grows.'

Mr. Pink stood upon the sands and held out his arms towards the fisherman.

He called out again.

The boat remained still as if painted into a picture of the sea, and the fisherman still slept.

When anxious agony possesses the human mind, even the sea, wide and watery as it is, appears sometimes to the trembling and tormented one to be indeed only a picture of waters and no real thing.

At that moment, with only one idea in his heart, and that idea to obtain help for his sister from the only one that Mr. Pink believed was able to give it, Mr. Roddy's agent fancied the wide sea to be a green highway that led to the sleeping fisherman. For—and in great distress one hardly knows what one does—Mr. Pink walked with his arms outstretched into the sea.

The boat had seemed so near, and the sea green and so like a firm carpet, that it certainly appeared natural to suppose that one could walk out to the boat and touch the fisherman's arm that lay so idly over the stern.

But history, that so often repeats itself, now, alas! did so again; for although he was not blind like the cow, yet when the waters flowed around him, and the boat that he sought disappeared behind the dark rock, Mr. Pink sank out of sight too, and was never seen again on the Mockery shore.

Chapter 17

A BROWN RIBBON

WHEN an untoward calamity falls upon the head of a meek one, its heavy stroke is often softened and turned, and the dread thing cheated of its blow, provided that a chance occurs to explain it away in a simple manner.

Miss Pink was one of those who, though fearing all things beforehand, take the most simple line of thought when anything terrible is said to have happened, for she would entirely disbelieve it. And although Mary Gulliver, who was in the field with her cows, had seen with her own eyes Mr. Pink walk into the sea and never return again to the shore, yet Miss Pink was just as sure that her brother had only gone for a sail with the fisherman—perhaps to the islands?

This idea of Miss Pink's was certainly strengthened because the day after Mr. Pink's disappearance the fisherman wasn't seen either.

This day was the first of July and high summer. The sky above Mockery was coloured at dawn like the inner petals of a splendid rose, and the small birds sang their early songs of praise to the wonderful founder of all summer days.

Had a wise one, whose wisdom might exceed in a small measure that of Mr. James Tarr, expected to see—and such a one is never disappointed—that the dwellers in the pretty gap upon this summer's day wore leopard-wise the same spots in their coats as ever, he would merely have remarked that Mr. Pink had gone as his colour foretold and invited him, and that the others would follow as their merry, mad, or sad destiny directed.

Mr. Pink, as Miss Ogle remarked in a letter to Mr. Roddy, should have taken a more practical view of his master's interest. He should have turned Mr. Gulliver out of his farm and let it to Mr. Cheney, who had a fine aptitude in adding house to house and field to field. 'And now'—and Miss Ogle invited herself to become Mr. Roddy's agent because Mr. Pink was gone—'here's a fine business,' she wrote, 'and under the wicked labour laws who's to drown him?—there's this fisherman settled in a cottage, an idler who catches crabs just when he wishes, and who lives without any character, and, as far as Mr. Pattimore can tell, without a name either.'

'Who is to tell,' Miss Ogle added, 'that the wicked life of this new fisherman might not prevent Mr. Cheney from following Mr. Tarr's wisely given hint and discovering those golden earrings under the green mound?' And so Miss Ogle ended her letter to Mr. Roddy.

There was something in this July day—for colour calls out sound sometimes—that caused

Mrs. Pring to rattle her pail more than she used to do on dismal and dull days; and she even stopped while scrubbing her doorstep to stare at the sea as if she expected the poor drowned body of Mr. Pink to step out of it and bow to her.

There is nothing like a July day—and this one happened to be a Saturday, too—to make all children born of the earth riotous with a spirit of naughtiness that is not unmixed with a merry malice. And so the Mockery brats, after rolling in the dust of the lane to sharpen their wits, began to follow Esther Pottle—who was now grown old enough to feel her own prettiness and so was growing more modest—who they supposed was out looking for the Nellie-bird.

But the fisherman not being in the way, the pack bethought them of Mr. Caddy, who had so often informed his ducks exactly—taking every detail of the adventure into consideration—how he would use a young and willing girl if she rested for a short five minutes upon the green clover near to his gate.

'Let's drive she to wold Caddy,' they cried. And so they did, and Esther, hot and flushed with running, fell almost into Mr. Caddy's arms, who was regarding with the wise, leisurely thoughts of a philosopher the green pond-weeds, now fully in flower, where the ducks were swimming.

Once safely there into the goat's mouth, Mockery, as represented by its children, crawled under a hedge that was near by and peered through the bushes. They hoped that Mr. Caddy, whose wife—or 'wold 'oman,' as they called her—was gone that day to Weyminster, would greet Esther's hot panting—for since the arrival of the fisherman she had bloomed and sprouted—with an indelicate gesture; and so they crawled nearer to watch. But—who would have thought it? —here was Mr. Caddy, a man known far and wide for his stories, an old idler who talked to his ducks, and now in a pretty corner garlanded and near covered by green bushes with a girl, more willing than a painted butterfly, and asking her whether she happened to have at home a brown ribbon suitable for his Sunday hat!

'I bain't one of they who despise churchgoing,' said Mr. Caddy gravely, as though church thoughts had been occupying his mind all that happy day. 'Though Mr. Pattimore be always talking of God an' 'is naughty ways. An' I do like to go tidy, an' a new ribbon to me hat will show that poor Caddy bain't all a bag stuffed wi' wickedness.'

Mockery peeped through the hedge, the little girls getting the nearest to the fun, and, whispering to the boys that the merriment would soon begin, they watched breathlessly.

Their expectations were indeed heightened and encouraged when Esther, raising her clothes a little, placed a very firm and nicely rounded leg upon the second bar of Mr. Caddy's gate; but strange to say, Mr. Caddy, who certainly at that moment should have looked at the girl, turned away and nodded at the ducks.

And then when Esther, with so much of her own warmth in it, showed him her garter, inquiring whether that was about the width he wished the ribbon to be, Mr. Caddy, to whom the garter appeared to be of no more importance than a lady's hair-ribbon, replied that it might be a little wider.

'I want they bad choir girls,' said Mr. Caddy with emphasis, 'to see that I be dressed.'

Esther fastened her garter again, this time resting upon the grassy bank.

The two might have been alone in Eden, for no voice or footstep was near. Esther lay right out, in the manner that she liked best to lie, on the cool grass, and looked up through the green bushes with her eyes half closed.

Mockery watched Mr. Caddy.

'Mrs. Moggs do sell hat ribbon, don't she?' inquired Mr. Caddy, looking at Esther as though she were a log of green wood cast at the wayside 'And wi' thik shilling,' he said, putting the coin upon the gate, 'that I did take for ducks' eggs, thee mid buy what I do require.'

Esther jumped up, ready enough for the errand now the money was come, and walked away quickly, tossing her head.

Mr. Caddy looked at the drake that was swimming in the pond. 'You an' I be different birds now,' he said composedly.

Mr. Caddy leant against his gate and waited; he hoped that there would be enough change out of his shilling to buy a mackerel for dinner, if the fisherman, who hadn't been seen all that morning, landed upon the Mockery beach with his basket.

Mockery crept away disappointed.

Chapter 18

SOMETHING HAPPENS

EVERY ONE—and no person in Mockery was a stranger to this hope—desires that one day something will happen that will exalt him above his neighbour in the eyes of the world.

This hope knits together the hearts of all people, though by means of this very desire each hopes to be grandly separate.

Every heart has this desire, and every man, woman, and child watches anxiously for something to happen that will fulfil it.

Death, that comes to all, gives a fillip to this hope. For although in life one may be scarcely noticed, in death, to be alone and so quiet, is in a village at least an honour that should never be underrated.

To only disappear, as Mr. Pink had done, provided perhaps a little talk as to whether the agent had sailed out with the fisherman and gone to America, but had given nothing grander than that.

Mrs. Moggs missed him, because she had always liked the way that he had come to her begging her to go to the beautiful sea.

Miss Pink, of course, missed him too, but she believed that the kind fisherman would one day tell her where her brother was, if not row her there too, and so she, though her sickness increased, was contented.

A July afternoon with the sun on high is God's kind blessing, for then all the tiny gnats can sing to Him tunefully with their wings, forgetting for the moment the hungry swallows in the hot sleepy air that surrounds them.

The scent of the warm wind, where green leaves and flowers are, and haply the sea, is sweet and lively with the divine love of the Lord of life, whose ways are eternal.

Every one in Mockery who had seen the new fisherman felt that he was the right being for such a day, and missed him; and as Esther said to Mrs. Moggs, when she bought Mr. Caddy his hat ribbon, that 'they mackerel be nice,' others thought so too.

Mr. Pattimore was one of them. For this afternoon, for no better reason than merely to look at the sky, he got away from the dining-room and from the Dean and stood in the garden. Mr. Pattimore looked upward, and there the sky was, sure enough, looking pleasantly mottled and in colour like the leg of a child who has been paddling in cold water.

Mr. Pattimore distinguished it from other skies as being a mackerel one; and remembering well enough how Rebecca had burnt the early-dinner potatoes, having run off after Simon about the time that they should have been taken up, Mr. Pattimore thought feelingly, his chaste ideas permitting it, that a fresh mackerel, corresponding in look to the pretty sky, would be pleasant for the late vicarage tea.

'Where is the fisherman?' inquired Mr. Pattimore of his wife, who was sitting in a garden chair and sewing.

Mrs. Pattimore leant over her work, perhaps to hide the tiny garment she was sewing, or else her own blushes.

'No one has seen him to-day,' Mrs. Pattimore replied, covering over what was in her lap with a very homely-looking stocking of her husband's.

Mr. Pattimore looked again at the sky, that was marked so . like a fine fresh mackerel. Mr. Pattimore sighed.

When any one is missed from a useful employment—poor Mr. Pink, being a mere servant of the great, does not count here— every one looks round to consider what has happened to him. Mrs. Pottle and Mrs. Pring— Mrs. Topple never looked up now—had noticed as well as their pastor the mackerel sky.

Mrs. Pottle expected mackerel not to fall like manna, but to be brought along in the fisherman's basket and to be sold to her, for so fine would the catch be at the surprisingly cheap rate of six for sixpence.

But her dinner-time, when the fish should have been set a-frying, was now past, and Mr. Pottle, unnoticed and almost unnoticeable, had come in from his garden and sniffed near to the fire as if he thought that something should have been frying there. But it was left to Mr. Gulliver, who being placed high upon his haystack could see things afar off, to notice—and with his world peopled with monsters he was ready enough to do so—a something strangely coloured upon the Mockery cliff.

Seeing Mr. Gulliver pause in his work and look towards some distant object that appeared to interest him, for he called to Mary, who began to look too, Mrs. Pottle allowed her eyes to go in the same direction to the Mockery cliff, where something coloured like a nosegay was resting.

'Do 'ee go and see who 'tis,' Mrs. Pottle called out to Esther, who was busy breaking some sticks that Dinah had fetched from the wood. 'Do 'ee go and see who 'tis, for I do believe 'tis thik Nellie-bird.'

Mrs. Pottle spoke the last word loudly and excitedly, and the pack of Mockery children, roving in search of mischief to do, caught it up and shouted, 'The Nellie-bird!'

Mr. Pattimore watched from his garden. 'Why,' he wondered, 'should those children that he had so carefully named, being all Peters or Pauls or Deborahs, run down from the hill as soon as they had climbed it, as though they had seen something that should never have been there?'

The children had climbed up there fast enough, and after staring for a moment at something upon the mound had scrambled down again, rolling over one another in heaps.

Mary Gulliver was the first to hear what they said as soon as they raced one another into the village, for she caught at once at the shouted words 'monkey' and 'naked,' and looked ashamed.

And now the children, who all called out in exactly the same voice, all the village over, 'that a naked ape all dressed in flowers was upon the cliff,' were heard by Mr. Pattimore, who looked too. What he saw determined him, for who but he, the pastor, should direct affairs now that something really wicked had come to Mockery? And who but he, when the evil appearance was defeated, should receive the reward—high preferment—a deanery?

So simply had event followed event at Mockery Gap, as generation followed generation, that nothing had ever occurred that caused so great an excitement as this new appearance.

Even those visitors who had come at the beginning of the hot and amorous summer weather had caused no such sensation of this dreadful kind. Mr. Tarr had but shaken, as he always liked to do, the everyday life by pointing out that the shadow was better than the substance, and so had brought Mrs. Topple to her knees and Miss Pink to her fears.

That was all well and proper, and set in the natural latitude of decorum, as Mr. Pink's disappearance, which could have happened to any one.

But here—and the children's yells were hushed as Mr. Pattimore strode out of his gate, taking the lane to the cliff—was another matter, a rare and wicked one, a strange beast.

Here in Mockery, as Mary Gulliver explained to Dinah and Rebecca, as they proceeded to the hill in the immediate wake of the minister, all nakedness should be covered, though not by summer flowers. 'If so be 'tis a man monkey,' the other Mary said, "e can't hide all of 'es self in honeysuckle, and they bad children did come down from hill calling out that Nellie-bird be the same as wold Caddy do tell 'is ducks of, that be one of Gulliver's demons.'

'Poor Simon won't fancy we a-watching,' said Dinah.

'Children bain't always right,' said Rebecca; 'they bain't Deans.'

'No,' said Mary, 'and a Dean be a man who bain't always like a monkey.'

Mr. Cheney walked with his son at a little distance from the others, as became a large farmer and a searcher for golden earrings. Miss Pink, who though she heard the cries, didn't go to see who it was, because she felt more than ever sure now that an answer would soon come to her letter, though perhaps not from Mr. Gulliver. So Miss Pink stayed at home, and dusted her front room, and prepared a dinner, in the fond hope that her brother might return from the islands, where she believed him gone with the fisherman, or that the answer to her letter might come before she died.

Mr. Gulliver walked near to Mrs. Cheney, who feared that one of her best cows, the one who supplied so much pocket-money for pretty God Simon, had been caught in a bush, like the ram in Genesis, by the horns.

Mr. Gulliver carried his map in his hand; every now and again he consulted it, supposing that it was the Great Cham of China, as yellow as an evening primrose, that had settled upon Mockery cliff.

The mound was indeed occupied, though by no yellow potentate, but merely by a large ape, who, feeling in a happy and joyous mood that afternoon, having escaped from his master at Maidenbridge, Mr. Dobbin, had come to Mockery and climbed the hill. And there he hung himself with honeysuckle and bryony and sat happy in the sun.

Mr. Pattimore, who let his black gown now fall to its full length—he had gathered it up a little when he climbed the hill—approached the mound.

'I believe your name should be Satan,' said Mr. Pattimore, looking up at the monkey, whose hair shone yellow in the sun, and whose body was covered by leaves and flowers.

The monkey grinned.

'Traitor, heady, high-minded, lover of pleasure,' called out Mr. Pattimore, remembering his last sermon; 'without natural affection, covetous, boaster, proud, blasphemous, fierce, incontinent, laden with sins.'

The monkey grinned again.

Around him quivered the burning glory of the sun. The whole heat of the heavens rested upon him, only to be delicately cooled when it touched the green leaves and the flowers.

Mr. Pattimore's words had little or no effect upon the creature who sat upon the mound, and so might have sat until the darkness of the night came; only, the rude Mockery children, after collecting many little heaps of Roddites, began to cast them up at him.

Mr. Pattimore would have turned away, leaving the matter to them, though their intention wasn't as righteous as he supposed, for the unseemly brats hoped the monkey would shake off the flowers in avoiding the shells. But as he was on the point of turning away, Mrs. Pattimore, who had been watching the scene with eyes downcast in modest manner, now left her husband, and climbing the mound stood in front of the creature as if to protect him from the shells and little stones.

Mr. Pattimore's first thought when he saw

her go from him was fierce anger; his second,
humiliation; his third, a wish that he had left
her in the laurels, taken away Dean Ashbourne's picture from his friend by force—and
married Miss Ogle.

After his thoughts had run so far, jealousy,
that fine parlour companion, entered into him,
and showed him his wedded lady as he had
not seen her for years, as a lovely woman.

And there she was, with her summer frock
that appeared to be near as thin as the monkey's
flowers, so near to the beast that she might
have touched him or he her.

Mr. Pattimore was upon the point of
climbing the mound in order to separate them
by force, when a diversion occurred that drew
off for a moment the interest of the onlookers,
so that the ape in one leap descended from the
mound and was gone. The new excitement
was caused by the tumultuous screams of
Esther Pottle, whom Master Simon Cheney
had discovered hiding behind, and indeed
entangled in, a gorse bush, very much as Mrs.
Cheney had expected her cow to be. Simon,
finding her there, had at once begun to carry
her off to an even more private place; while
Esther, for some strange cause that the future
must alone disclose, resisted.

Simon, it seems, as well as Mr. Pattimore,
had taken that very afternoon the first step in
the tortuous path of jealousy; for having gently

suggested to each of the three older maids that they might one or all retire with him down a leafy lane that was near by, each had replied that she wished to remain looking at the pretty flowers upon the monkey. Simon turned with displeasure, and bidding them go to hell, which wasn't particularly polite of him, he wandered amongst the green bushes and discovered Esther.

The pack of children no sooner saw that the ape was gone and a girl running, than they contented themselves with the final excitement of chasing her home, with their usual mocking calls about the Nellie-bird, and what she and he did together when they met.

Mr. Pattimore followed slowly in their steps, looking down at the ground.

Mrs. Pattimore walked behind.

When all was still upon the downs, the fisherman, who had gone early that morning to buy a new net, appeared from behind the mound and descended into the green lane and so to the summer sea, to prepare his nets and lines for a night's fishing.

Chapter 19

THE END OF MR. DOBBIN

IN order to discover how the yellow monkey escaped and got to dancing upon Mockery cliff, so raising a strange jealousy in the heart of Mr. Pattimore, and a certainty in Mr. Gulliver's heart that his map was a true one, we must go back a few months to Mr. Dobbin.

After the stormy night, when the waves had reached so high that they broke Mr. Dobbin's boat that he had dragged up the shore as far as he was able, Mr. Dobbin as soon as it was light left the snug shelter of his hut to look at the angry waves.

Although Mr. Dobbin had never read those wonderful tales called the Arabian Nights, he was certainly as superstitious and as willing to accept an omen as any fisher of the River Tigris.

The evil genius of the sea had broken his boat, given him but a sorry living, and often near drowned him. Mr. Dobbin looked at the sea and wondered if any sign would come to bid him leave it for ever.

The very high tide that had broken his boat had now carried the sea a long way from the shore. The waves roared in the same uncomfortable manner as they had done in the night, but they were retired to some little distance. Mr. Dobbin looked at the Blind Cow Rock;

he could if he chose walk to it along a path of seaweed.

Upon the rock there was a yellow ape, that amused itself by pulling pieces of seaweed from the sides of the rock to dress itself.

The sea, thought Mr. Dobbin, had at last given him something, but it was a present that decided Mr. Dobbin that he must leave at once. The ape must have leapt from a passing ship.

Mr. Dobbin knew the character of the Mockery children; once when he had caught a few fish they had rushed upon him and upset his basket. If they met the monkey they would stone it to death. Mr. Dobbin was friendly to beasts and birds. He recollected a few remarks of a Mockery boy, Master Toby, about the owls in the tall trees near to the church. 'They should all be killed,' Toby had remarked, looking up at an owl upon a branch. 'Why, what hurt do they do?' inquired Mr. Dobbin. Toby put both hands to his mouth in the manner of a king's trumpeter and shouted through them; he was calling the pack. 'Owls do no harm,' said Mr. Dobbin. 'They do peck holes in the trees, and should all be killed,' shouted Toby, picking up a stone and throwing it into the tree. Mr. Dobbin said no more....

He now went to the ape, who allowed itself to be led with a string to the fisherman's hut.

Mr. Dobbin departed that night, and Mr.

Gulliver, who took him to Maidenbridge in his light waggon, asked no questions as to what he carried in it.

Mr. Dobbin, who had been imbued while at Mockery with certain ideas of Mr. Pattimore, named his monkey Paul.

He hired a small room in the town, fed Paul upon a basin of bread-and-milk, and slept contentedly because the sea was so far away.

The next day Mr. Dobbin went forth into the town to look for work.

Mr. Dobbin walked through the town gardens; he wondered whether he should visit Mr. Tarr, whose house was near to them. Mr. Dobbin shuddered; he thought he wouldn't go to him, for hadn't Mr. Tarr sent him out of his garden and advised him to go a-fishing!

The town gardens were quiet enough, but the streets were busy.

One of the chief faults that Mr. Dobbin always had to find with the sea was the noise it made; it hardly ever seemed, even upon a moderately calm day, to be quite still and quiet. Once away from it, with Paul, he expected to find quiet behaviour everywhere. But Mr. Dobbin was disappointed. Unfortunately, he had chosen a market-day to look for work and to find a new master. The noise in the main street of Maidenbridge was as ill-mannered as the noise of the sea. Everywhere there was confusion and shouting. Dealers called their wares from their stalls in the street, cheap-jacks shouted, and dogs barked. As soon as Mr. Dobbin found himself in the midst of all the clamour, a large bull broke loose from the market and charged up the street, its mouth foaming and its eyes gleaming with red fury. Mr. Dobbin had never at its worst seen the sea look so mad and furious. The bull was followed by a mild policeman, who waved a handkerchief that was, alas! a red one. The bull turned and gored the policeman to death. After so doing it charged of its own accord into the slaughter-house.

As soon as the bull was gone, Mr. Dobbin found himself standing outside the corn exchange. Two farmers were disputing about the quality of a sample of barley. They both grew as angry as the bull. One threw the sample in the face of the other, who replied with a stout blow. Mr. Dobbin passed just at the moment, and received the blow in his chest.

Mr. Dobbin turned and tried to walk upon the pavement, hoping still to find some one that he might ask for employment.

A crowd of young women, who were shouting, singing, and laughing, were rushing along the pavement after a young man almost as wildly as the bull had rushed at the policeman with the red handkerchief. They pushed Mr. Dobbin rudely into the road.

A large car came by and knocked him back upon the pavement again. Mr. Dobbin sought refuge in a narrow blind alley that reminded him a little of a cave that he had once sheltered in beside the Mockery sea.

He had always wished for a master to control the sea, and now he wished for one to control Maidenbridge upon a market-day. He would gladly work for such a master if he could be found. Here was turbulence and noise, worse than he had been used to, worse than the turbulence of the sea. He was glad that he had shut his room door upon Paul and so left him safe and away from the noise.

Mr. Dobbin peeped out from his shelter.

Every one in the town seemed to be guided by the same rude and unmannerly forces that had guided the waves that Mr. Dobbin had felt so strong against him when he went a-fishing. Everywhere there was noise and con-fusion, nowhere was there calm and quiet. Certainly here was no place for Mr. Dobbin to find the right master.

From his retreat, Mr. Dobbin now noticed that a little further down the street there was a pause in the clamour. A few people were standing in groups and watching a house in silence. Mr. Dobbin joined them. Before the door of the house a hearse was waiting. In a little while a coffin was borne out of the house and placed silently in the hearse. Mr.

Dobbin watched gratefully. He saw order and quiet come at last amongst all the noise and shouting. The hearse was driven slowly to the cemetery, and Mr. Dobbin followed it cheerfully. Within the walls of the cemetery all was harmony and quiet. The manager of the town burial board was there to watch; he was a little gentleman in a frock-coat, with a bald head, who liked funerals.

When all was over, Mr. Dobbin addressed himself to Mr. Best, the manager, in a low tone that became the place. The manager drew him to one side, so that they might not interrupt a lady, the only daughter of her father, who was kneeling beside the new grave and praying.

'You seem to serve the best of masters here, sir,' said Mr. Dobbin, 'a master who is even better than Mr. James Tarr; would you be so kind as to tell me his name so that I may ask him for work?'

'Death is our master,' replied Mr. Best, 'and I allow no loud talking.'

'You never allow children in here, who throw stones or shout?' inquired Mr. Dobbin, who wished to make sure that the work there would suit him.

The manager held up his hands in astonishment. 'The children who come here,' he said, 'when there's scarlet fever in the town, never throw stones.'

Mr. Best regarded Mr. Dobbin for some moments in silence. Mr. Dobbin liked Mr. Best; he liked the quiet way he looked at everything.

'We have just buried our under gardener,' said Mr. Best, 'who was a very silent man.'

Mr. Dobbin explained that he had once worked in that capacity for Mr. Tarr.

'You may have our under gardener's place if you choose,' said Mr. Best, taking off his hat and holding it in both his hands as the lady, rising from her knees, walked by weeping.

'I hope to give satisfaction,' whispered Mr. Dobbin.

'I hope you will,' replied Mr. Best. 'And be so good as to remember, Dobbin, that no dog or boy or anything that disturbs our quiet is permitted to enter here.'

Mr. Dobbin bowed; he must, he decided, keep Paul very close in his room.

'And now,' said Mr. Best, 'I will show you our pleasure-grounds.'

Mr. Best led Mr. Dobbin around the cemetery; he led him with pride. Nothing was out of place or untidy; the little worms in the grass were silent, all was trim and neat.

After going around the paths, Mr. Best stood upon the chapel steps and surveyed the scene.

'Nothing disturbs our peace here,' said Mr.

Best; 'our guests are all silent ones, and whatever noise they made before they came, they are quiet now.'

'Perhaps,' inquired Mr. Best of Mr. Dobbin, 'you have seen a country churchyard?'

Mr. Dobbin replied that he had.

'But you may not know,' said the manager archly, 'that people, whenever they can afford our fees and the doctors, come into the town to die.'

'I can well believe it, sir,' said Mr. Dobbin.

Mr. Dobbin left the cemetery in company with Mr. Best, who advised him the nearest way by a quiet back street to his room.

For a while all went well, and no one was happier in his employment than Mr. Dobbin. But however quietly a man may live and labour, and however good a master he may serve, nothing can prevent ill luck, if such be his destiny, from following his steps. Alas! for now we come to why the yellow ape was seen at Mockery again, and consistently haunted the village until at last by a sad fatality Paul was drowned.

The matter happened like this. Toby, the Mockery boy who blamed the owls for pecking holes in the trees, wished to find Mr. Dobbin, who had, it appeared, taken the part of the owls, in order to tell him that he and the other rude children had stoned three of them to death. Master Toby having gone

to Maidenbridge with the Norbury carrier to
visit his grandmother, inquired after Mr.
Dobbin and discovered his room.

He found the door locked, but unfortunately
Mr. Dobbin, who had felt more than usually
pleased that day, because the head gardener
had died and he was to have his place, had left
the key in the door.

Toby unlocked and opened the door, saw
the monkey, and ran away....

No one took a greater pride in the funerals
that occurred at the Maidenbridge cemetery
than Mr. Best. And so one can well suppose
that when the head gardener's coffin was carried
to the new-dug grave, Mr. Best felt that a
hideous indignity was offered to him and his
because a large ape had jumped upon the coffin
and was being carried too—and some one
laughed.

Mr. Best, losing his temper for the first
time in his life, attacked the offender with his
umbrella. Paul danced away over the tombs.
Mr. Best followed. The clergyman smiled.
The monkey ran to Mr. Dobbin, who was
trimming a grave. Mr. Best demanded of
Mr. Dobbin whether the beast was his.

Mr. Dobbin looked at the graves around
him. He couldn't bear to leave them; he
couldn't bear to be sent away.

He said he knew not the ape.

Mr. Best struck at Paul with his umbrella,

and together with stones and blows he and Mr. Dobbin drove it from the cemetery.

Mr. Dobbin went home sadly; he grieved for Paul; he couldn't forgive himself for denying him. In a few months' time Mr. Best advertised for a new head gardener—Mr. Dobbin was dead.

When he was beaten from the cemetery poor Paul bethought him of his first home and fled to Mockery.

Chapter 20

MR. PATTIMORE SEES A VISION

At the tea-table the evening after Mr. Dobbin's ape was discovered upon Mockery cliff, Mr. Pattimore stared hard at the fine and full-length portrait, dressed in all his grandeur, of Dean Ashbourne. He stared so hard that a piece of bread-and-butter that he was taking to his mouth touched his nose. This error occurred because the Dean that he looked at had suddenly become a blushing lady guarding an ape.

Mr. Pattimore felt that in order to forgive the fisherman, whom he blamed for the monkey's presence in the village, he must give the fisherman a name. What should the fisherman be called? The rude children called him the Nellie-bird, a strange creature whose existence had been noted in the natural history of the world; but that was little better than a pagan title, and utterly unsuited to one whom Mr. Pattimore hoped to both name and preach into chastity.

Mr. Pattimore doubted very much whether the fisherman had ever been baptized. He could hardly believe that he had been. The taking himself away when he should have been fishing had but aggravated the usual lazy behaviour of the man. But with a name, a pretty and a proper one, the fisherman would no doubt fulfil his vocation in going down to the sea to fish instead of bringing apes to the hills to awake a husband's jealousy.

Whenever he chose a name for any child who was going to be christened, Mr. Pattimore would slyly visit Mr. Pring, the church clerk and sexton, and ask him to so deal with the parents, by means of a simple present of a half-crown, that they would allow one of the names to be a Bible one, which would ensure—Mr. Pattimore felt certain of it—at least a little more than the usual attention from above.

It was Mr. Pattimore's custom to say his prayers before he retired to rest in the dining-room. He would pray, looking up at the Dean, to follow in his steps; and this evening he asked God to be kind enough to tell him—if convenient—the best name to call the fisherman.

Mr. Pattimore never liked to go to bed. His nature, that he had beaten down with the heavy hammer of St. Paul's doctrine, had originally been, before his ambitions had coveted a dean's honours, a mild and soft one. And even now the flesh, hammered as he had hammered it, and flattened out and shamed into quietude, kicked at times.

He couldn't help feeling uncomfortable when he passed his wife's bedroom door, before climbing the steeper stairs to his attic.

He never dared to peep in upon her, but however quietly he went by she always heard

him, and her good-night couldn't fail to
remind him of something. This remembrance would meet him upon the landing
where her door was and look at him; or rather,
he would look at it, as upon a picture that
he had to see.

A tiny hollow in a grassy cliff, and Nellie—
for she had been Nellie until the honeymoon
was over—Nellie looking up at him.

He wore his clerical garments, but she was
in white.

The little blue butterflies were merry that
day and the grasshoppers. Mr. Pattimore
had looked at her. She hid her eyes from his
and pouted. Mr. Pattimore took off his coat!
She should have said 'No,' she should have
pointed out to him the ship in the bay, she
should have called out that there was a rabbit
in the grass, instead of breaking off the green
seed-pod of a yellow-horn poppy and throwing
it at him. . . .

Mr. Pattimore would hurry by the landing,
but the good-night and the vision of the poppy,
the blue butterflies and the white wantonness,
all Nellie then, always met him.

He reached the attic at last, though with his
heart quivering, and lay in his bed.

And now, whichever way he turned, and
even though his eyes were tightly shut, he saw
the ape dressed in flowers and his wife standing
beside him.

Although his eyes were shut, Mr. Pattimore felt sure that the devil by some means or other was entering into him.

The summer night was very still, and the stars seen through the widely open attic window shone warm.

There was a sound somewhere. Was it by means of that sound that the devil had got him?

He ought, he felt, to have prayed longer in the dining-room, then God might have filled his mind with a wide circle of Bible names out of which he could choose one for the fisherman.

Mr. Pattimore listened. Had the vision, that he always saw near where her room was, followed him up his steep stairs?

Mr. Pattimore sat up. He heard the midnight sea, the wicked one, the beautiful, the inspirer of a huge wickedness; he heard the sea. However much he had shut out from him all the gentle longings of his loving lady, this sound would come in. It came from the dark places of love, out of the bottom of the sea.

It came naked, it stood before him as he had stood before her, as Milton's Adam new learned in love, in that pretty corner of the cliff where the blue butterflies were.

He saw it as she must have seen him, through her fingers—all the male nakedness of the sea.

Dark movements were upon it, that came

into him with the sound. Dark movements, the purple blossoms of the deep making their music.

The sound rose and fell, and Mr. Pattimore listened.

The ground swell splashed upon the Blind Cow Rock.

Mr. Pattimore bit his finger to keep the noise away. He turned over and slept.

Chapter 21

FISH TO PLEASE A NELLIE

MR. PATTIMORE awoke early; he looked through the window at the sky.

The dawn had broken shyly, like a young dark-eyed girl who first thinks of love. So this summer dawn thought of the new day.

Mr. Pattimore saw that the sky was again spotted with little clouds, as it had been the afternoon before.

Mr. Pattimore awoke hungry, and the look of the sky reminded him at once of mackerel and the fisherman.

He rose from his bed, full of the idea of converting the fisherman and giving him a name. 'If the fisherman,' he thought, 'is given a fitting name to suit his occupation, out of the Bible, then he would no more idle in the lanes, but would go out in his boat and catch the fish.'

A summer's morning, although it gave that pretty writer Charles Lamb a headache, always pleased Mr. Pattimore. Its soft colours he could look at without fear, because these gentle colours were not upon his wife's cheeks; and he could watch the flowers and the sweet airs of heaven kiss one another, in all chastity and godliness.

The early morning filled Mr. Pattimore's heart with hope and happiness.

He saw Mockery—fair Mockery—coloured by his hope. All the meadows and lanes about him, and the wood, looked to him like the interior of the vast church where he as the principal figure walked with the gentle and easy gait of a monarch, and might if he wished rest upon any dewy and grassy bank as if it were a cushioned throne.

The early birds sang as well as any little boys in a choir, and the colours that Mr. Pattimore saw about him were as fine, or nearly so, as the decorated interior of any cathedral.

And best of all, to Mr. Pattimore's senses came the feeling of chastity—the chaste dawn. He felt that this holy aspect of things seen would at least govern for many hours the rudeness of the day. Mr. Pattimore's thoughts had soared, as well they might do upon such a morning, as high as the lark's, and he let himself out of his own gate into the road with no other thoughts in his mind than chaste holiness.

But the earth isn't heaven, and Mr. Pattimore hadn't walked four paces before all his nice thoughts were shattered at a blow, and that a sudden one.

Upon a bank, at the entrance of a little lane, and under a fine spreading chestnut tree, God Simon was pressing Mary Gulliver—who was excitedly resisting him—wrathfully against the yellow flowers, and was complaining as he held her pantingly—which complaint even Mr. Pattimore saw no call for—that all the Mockery maidens were forsaking him and were running after the fisherman.

Mr. Pattimore stood and shook with anger; the bubble that had been the dawn was now rudely burst, and the fair skies became to him a mere roof to a horrid kennel.

Simon turned, and, seeing Mr. Pattimore, released Mary, who went down the lane to fetch the cows, a little hot and tumbled, with a parting word to Simon that she would tell her father.

Simon had expected that, and so, in order to make things clearer to the clergyman and to excuse himself too, he remarked sulkily:

"'Tis thik b . . . fisherman, that do set maidens against I; they be all after 'e now, and none of we can touch a hair of them, wi'out a father being named, or else fisherman.'

Mr. Pattimore remembered what he had come out to do.

'But the fisherman has no name,' he said.

"'E bain't nothing, only a Nellie-bird,' replied Master Simon, going past the vicarage hoping to meet Rebecca, who would naturally be coming about that time to her work.

Mr. Pattimore took the path to Mr. Pring's cottage. Though the chastity of the morning had been shattered by what he had seen, 'yet perhaps if he named the fisherman wisely all might yet be well.'

'It might be,' thought Mr. Pattimore, 'this fisherman with the pagan name that Mr. Tarr had so unthinkingly bestowed upon him, according to the accepted opinion of the village, who was perverting Mockery. That view of the fisherman as a wanton must have been the cause of his own lighting upon a sin at his very gates and in the eyes of the chaste dawn.'

Mr. Pattimore found Mr. Pring, who was an early riser, milking his lame cow in his little field that was shaded on one side by a high hedge and on the other by a pretty grove of larch trees. The pleasant morning had now healed Mr. Pattimore of his shock, and he approached Pring silently and spoke to him.

It was fortunate for Mr. Pring that he held firmly between his knees the bucket into which the milk was flowing, or else the fright of Mr. Pattimore's sudden arrival, and the gentleman's remarking so suddenly at six o'clock that he had come out in the hope of naming the new fisherman, might have caused the entire loss of the milk his cow had given him.

'They children,' said Mr. Pring, when he had recovered himself a little, 'that do shout wild in village do name 'e the Nellie-bird.'

Mr. Pattimore moved back a pace or two and looked thoughtfully at the sea. The Blind Cow Rock, dark in all the sparkle and

shine of the water, reminded him of something
—a whale.

'I might call him Jonah,' said Mr. Pattimore, coming nearer to Pring again.

'Were 'e a fisherman?' the road-mender
asked.

'Yes,' replied Mr. Pattimore, 'in a kind of
way he was, though the fish devoured him.'

'The poor man did bait hook wi' 'is own
self; but did thik fish ever get to shore?'

'No, never,' said Mr. Pattimore.

Mr. Pring rose from his stool; he placed
the milk for safety at a little distance and began
to rub his cow's back with his hand. The cow
lowered her head gratefully; she was pleased
with this kind attention from her master.

A clatter of buckets came from the cottage;
Mrs. Pring had come out of her door to feed
the pigs.

Mr. Pattimore turned to the sea. The sun,
whose kingdom is the earth, blessed his people.
The sun broke through the little clouds and
soaked Mockery in a bath of glory.

Mr. Pattimore and Pring both looked at
the Blind Cow Rock at the same instant. A
tall man stood upon the rock, who appeared
about to cast a net into the sea.

''Tis Jonah,' said Mr. Pring, 'an' 'tain't
no whale 'e do try to catch this morning, but a
mackerel.'

Mr. Pattimore had awakened hungry, and

the early morning air, now that he was out in it, made him wish more than ever for a good breakfast. He could see even the Dean smiling from his frame when a fine fish, nicely fried by Rebecca, would be uncovered ready to taste; and then he wouldn't want so much to look—poor man—at Mrs. Pattimore's summer clothes.

Mr. Pattimore bid Mr. Pring good morning. He took the way to the sea. He walked excitedly, for perhaps—and who knows what a good God intends for His servants?—he might purchase a fish as well as name the fisher.

As Mr. Pattimore approached the waves, the same call of beauty and all loveliness that had attracted his wife earlier in the season now attracted him too. The flowers had led her, the summer sounds led him. The sunlight danced and quivered upon the moving surface of the sea, the ripple or the tiny summer waves made happy music, while a three-masted barque, as if it knew the eyes of man wished it to be there, traversed the cool morning waters, with wide sails spread. A white sea-gull flew so low that it almost touched the ripples with its wings.

Mr. Pattimore walked upon the cool yellow sands.

He was conscious as he walked that the sands were shining. He looked quickly up at the blue sky, but found it shining too.

Nothing—not all the deans in the world—could now prevent a truth overtaking his steps. He walked amid beauty—perfect beauty—and remembered that his wife had once been called Nellie. He clapped his hands to take his mind away from that word. 'Dorcas,' he called, 'Dorcas.'

Mr. Pattimore looked into the sea: a great many tiny fishes were swimming in it; these were followed by a shoal of mackerel, that often in their hungry endeavour to get a little fish leaped out of the water.

Mr. Pattimore was so intent upon watching the deep blue of the sea, the shining pebbles, and the little fish, that he was near descending into it in order to become eternal beauty at one fling as Mr. Pink had done, when he happened to notice that near to him was the new fisherman, without his cap, with his hair and beard shining in the sun, pulling in his net.

Mr. Pattimore went at once to his aid, and they pulled together in all comradeship. The net was very heavy and near ready to break, for it was filled with shining and glittering fish.

At his earnest request the fisherman filled a basket full of fish for Mr. Pattimore—for a shilling. And what with one thing and another, what with the excitement of the nakedness of the morning, and the excitement of seeing so many fish taken, Mr. Pattimore forgot that he had come down to the sea to name the fisherman.

And he also forgot 'Dorcas.' For as he went off with his filled basket he said happily, 'Nellie will enjoy these for her breakfast.'

Chapter 22

MR. CADDY SETS A SNARE

No woman, even if we may take Dr. John Donne's interpretation of them to be true, can change her face and show so great a depth of hidden cunning as the sea.

The sea is such a variable companion, when one goes down to it, that at certain times we are almost startled by the alterations in its countenance, that seem strangely to correspond to the quick and fretful changes in the human mind.

Under the shadow of a heavy thunder-cloud, it becomes the wine-dark deep as Homer saw it. But seen again with the afternoon sun upon it, it becomes a Victorian lady, until the tide creeps unnoticed around our feet, and we remember the days of Canute and his fine flatterers, that were, after all, exactly the same pretty gentlemen as the flatterers who live now. And when we have climbed out of the way of the water and are safely seated upon a higher ridge of pebbles, and look again at the sea, it isn't the same. The sea is no recorder of history now; it has become pure emotion. The sea moans and weeps, shines and laughs, and tells as we gaze a little sadly at it a story of fair love passages: how a fair lady of noble presence stands upon the little rounded pebbles, and takes the hand of a bold fisherman who steps on shore from his boat; and his rough outer garments blowing apart, there is revealed the golden shift of a king.

And then as the light of day wanes and the darkness gathers, and we behold the far reaches of the deep, we are led to contemplate the grand vista of eternity. Then the dark waters gather tumultuously about the golden gate of the grave, behind which stands the Name, spoken with holy dread by all generations of mankind.

Spoken with awe unfathomable. For whatever we may think of the injustice, the cruelty, the pain here upon earth, the Name, and the terror and love of it that hides so silent behind the tomb, must for ever hide, too, the ultimate truth. God, for ever and everlasting, life without end—God.

Mr. Caddy wasn't of a jealous nature; he would stand beside his gate and tell the ducks that he didn't mind how often the Mockery girls went out to amuse themselves. 'All groves and meadows be box-beds wi' they maidens,' he would remark happily, knowing well enough that Simon or the girls would tell him all about it, and that he would have the pleasure of handing on all that they had said to the ducks.

However little the American nation may be able to agree here, I must be brave enough to venture the opinion that there is a type of human creature, godlike in nature, who can become very important to his environment by doing nothing. Mr. Caddy had become so, and the importance that he had in Mockery was shared by his ducks.

Mr. Caddy was by nature friendly to the world, though one person resident in it, though not of Mockery, had incurred his displeasure. This was none other than the Mr. Hunt who so frightened Mrs. Moggs when he came to her, talking about money.

Coming by in his motor one day, Mr. Hunt had run over one of Mr. Caddy's ducks that had become separated from the others and was quacking in the lane. Mr. Caddy did indeed walk as far as the duck and raise it pityingly, and it died in his arms.

The car was gone, and Mr. Hunt with it. Mr. Caddy carried the duck back to the pond and placed it gently upon the floating weeds.

And then he went back to his gate again and stared at the dead duck in the pond.

Mr. Hunt had made an enemy.

But little did the postmaster know how important Mr. Caddy was. Now listen. Mrs. Topple would always choose to pass Mr. Caddy's cottage on her way to the fields, and now that July was so near to running into August she would inquire of him as from an expert in botany where he supposed she might be able to find the clover with four leaves.

Mr. Caddy advised her to let the fields alone, and to begin to search, as she had finished with the children's lessons, by the roadside.

'But do 'ee mind Mr. Hunt don't kill 'ee,' remarked Mr. Caddy.

Every one in Mockery always wished that God had invented a way to increase the souls to be saved without there having to be children.

'I do often think,' said Mr. Caddy, who, before he learned how pleasant his gate was to lean against, had in his extreme youth been a rabbit-catcher—'I do often think that if they babies, that so soon be running children, had to bolt out of holes into rabbit netting, 'twould be better for all.'

'But dogs mid have they,' said Mrs. Pottle, who was passing down the lane, 'or else they ferrets Simon Cheney do keep in 's bag.'

'If they did,' said Mr. Caddy, after turning over in his mind the hard problem and looking at it from another angle—'if they did, 'twouldn't be noticed.'

As though they arose because Mr. Caddy had mentioned them, the children, the very worst among them—indeed, they might well have lived in those cities of the plain—surrounded Mr. Caddy and shouted to him that if he didn't say where the Nellie-bird had gone to they would stone his ducks to death, as surely and certainly as Mr. Hunt had killed the one he ran over.

'The fisherman,' said Mr. Caddy, addressing not the bad children but his good ducks, 'be where Esther Pottle do bide.'

The children with this news in their ears at once broke and ran, nearly overturning their teacher, who, following Mr. Caddy's advice, was already beginning to search the roadside for clover to heal her wound.

They ran here and there, that fair summer morning, for their holidays were begun, and they had nothing to do that day, save mischief.

Near to Mr. Gulliver's cottage they saw Esther. Mr. Gulliver was telling her how he had in the spring-time—and he had never forgotten it—seen an odd monster in the wood—a demon, he called it—who had in a moment of time, a miraculous moment, changed into her cousin Dinah and Master Simon Cheney.

Mr. Gulliver stood aside when the children ran by, and Esther, being unable to turn back and go to her home, fled to the sea.

But of all places to run to in the wide world, when one is being chased by the little sharp-toothed wolves, the sea is least likely to be a preserver; unless one means to dive after the precious pearl of eternity like Mr. Pink.

But Esther's faith in the fisherman was so strong, that had his boat been a mile from land instead of a yard or two she would have felt she was saved.

As it was, the fleeing Esther, near blinded by

her own hair, a pretty thing in the sun, with her frock unfastened by running, cast herself into the boat, and the fisherman pushed off.

Mockery perceiving this act of escape, gave the cries that dogs do when a doe rabbit, whose soft fur they had hoped to get their teeth into, has run into a deep hole in the ground that is beyond their reach.

The pack of Mockery had one voice, and their cries were accompanied by stones, that dropped into the sea about the boat, safe within which Esther had sunk exhausted upon the fisherman's nets.

'Wold Caddy do tell 'is ducks,' shouted the rude children, 'that every fisherman's boat wi' a maiden in en be a fine feather-bed.'

'Bad Esther, whose mother bain't married, be in thee's boat,' they shouted again, hoping to raise enough virtue in the heart of the fisherman to give him cause for throwing Esther into the sea.

'And mind blind cow don't watch 'ee.'

The fisherman stood beside his mast and smiled upon the children, while Esther, whose eyes matched the darkest deeps in colour, though a little dimmed now by love, looked up at the fisherman with all the faith and affection of a happy child.

The summer wind, that had ruffled the waters a little now, sank entirely into a dead calm. The boat's sail flapped or else hung limp, the tiny waves splashed upon the pebbles, and the children wandered away from the shore, crying out every now and again, in order to make their path the easier, 'The Nellie-bird! —the Nellie-bird!'

Chapter 23

MR. PATTIMORE FINDS HIS
KITE

SOMETHING happened to Mr. Pattimore after eating the fish that he helped the fisherman to catch.

For at table, instead of looking up at the grand portrait, he would sometimes steal a hidden look at his wife's shoe.

But not naughtily, and only in the manner of one who likes to think that there is anything both young and lovely in the world.

That peep carried Mr. Pattimore a little further perhaps from the Dean and all his chaste ideas than the good man intended to be carried. And when he uttered one afternoon in the presence of his wife, who was sewing a suspicious-looking garment—for she had now ceased to hide her work—the word 'children,' Mrs. Pattimore let fall her garment and blushed at the daisies. Alas! the blush soon faded, for Mr. Pattimore, speaking more to the green trees than to her—for they were sitting in the garden—remarked that ever since Mr. Pink had gone—and he feared the man might be dead —Miss Pink had asked him to try to do something to quiet the children.

'They shout out such funny words in the lanes that they make me afraid,' Miss Pink had told him.

'I am afraid,' said Miss Pink, 'of something I don't see.'

Mrs. Pattimore looked down at the daisies.

'I want to do something for the children,' her husband said. 'Their names don't carry them far to heaven, and I would like to help them.'

'Give them your kite,' said Mrs. Pattimore.

Mr. Pattimore didn't answer her for a moment, but he looked at his wife—and blushed.

His kite, that he had brought with him when he first came to Mockery, had for all the years that he had been there hung in the great wardrobe in the best bedroom, that was his wife's.

Mr. Pattimore didn't look at the window of the dining-room in which was the portrait, but at the inland cliff.

'Mrs. Moggs says,' said Mr. Pattimore, wishing to bring more reasons to help the idea of his kite-flying than Miss Pink's nervousness, 'that the children rush into her shop in a crowd and demand sweets as though they were robbers; and when she shows them her pretty white mice they merely cry out that they're not Nellie-birds.'

'Yes,' said Mrs. Pattimore, looking up at him, 'and Mr. Gulliver says that he believes they worship the devils that live in Newfoundland.'

'Remember Dean Ashbourne,' remarked Mr. Pattimore sternly, in order to stop his wife from talking and himself from forgetting the desire of his life.

He still thought himself safe, and when he left her to go and fetch the kite—though she offered to go instead of him—he walked with the firm step of one who, though married, lives as if he were not.

On his way upstairs he wondered why he had not let her go instead of him. With each step he grew more and more nervous; he felt that to enter her room was to go into the very bowels of temptation. He stopped upon the landing and hesitated. He might even now go to the landing window and lean out and call meekly, 'My dear, perhaps you had better after all fetch the kite, for I do not know where to find it.'

He stepped to the window, looking out with the intention of calling to her, but her chair under the window was empty, and she was standing beside the garden hedge talking to Miss Pink, who was in the lane, and asking her how her pain was.

Miss Pink's pale face was looking up at hers, frightened.

'I must find the kite myself,' Mr. Pattimore decided.

He hadn't visited his wife's bedroom since the morning when he saw his sin in loving her so devotedly and—he knew it then—so naughtily.

To continue in that way was, he knew, the very thing that the Dean—godly man!—blamed the world for—this continuous married wantonness.

'Fornication,' the good man would remark to his friends at Oxford, 'can never be so heinous, because it's damned in the act, whereas this—even good men sometimes speak well of.'

Mr. Pattimore remembered how he had followed the Dean's manners and wishes so soon after he took the girl, and he almost shouted out even now with shame when he remembered how he had once been naked in a field.

'But I'm not even a rector yet,' thought Mr. Pattimore, and moved excitedly to her bedroom door.

He opened the door hurriedly, making a great deal of noise, in order to frighten all temptation away, and, looking neither to the right hand nor to the left, he went direct to the wardrobe and opened it.

Mr. Pattimore stepped back.

The white frock hung there, the very one that had looked so transparent when she rested upon the dry grass that day upon the cliff.

He must touch it now as he touched it then. No, hardly like that!—because the place the kite was hidden in was behind the frock.

Mr. Pattimore had discovered by much practice a simple way of life, that Mr. Moody

the noted postman of Madder had always followed—that of putting an ugly thing in his
eye, instead of a pretty one.

And so now—and he did it manfully—he
forced himself to think of the pretty frock as
though it were a garment of Mrs Pottle's—a
woman Mr. Pattimore immensely disliked—
that he had once seen hanging upon a hedge,
and that even Mr. Caddy hadn't the hardihood
to stare at.

'Mrs. Pottle's,' he said, 'Mrs. Pottle's
petticoat. The kite must be here somewhere.'
Mr. Pattimore searched for it. He began to
move other garments, though without troubling
himself to think of them as Mrs. Pottle's
because they were such little ones. But in
order to get to the kite he was forced to put
them to one side.

As he did so, he saw what they were—all
tiny things that infant children use, and sewn
with stitches that any Arab would have envied.

Mr. Pattimore, looking at these pretty
things, wondered what they had to do with her.

'She is my wife,' said Mr. Pattimore. His
thoughts went out of him and crept queerly
backwards.

But why in his thoughts did she wear her
wedding frock?

And now here were these baby clothes.

Mr. Pattimore tore the kite from the bottom
of the wardrobe, and fled.

Chapter 24

MOCKERY WOOD

IT was a simple fact, and only Mrs. Topple
hadn't noticed it, that the fisherman—and
some there were who said he wasn't as young
as he looked—could be sad as well as careless.

Once he had been seen—by Esther, who felt
the sight so that she couldn't help telling Mrs.
Moggs about it—sitting upon the Blind Cow
Rock, during a low tide when the rock could
be reached without wetting one's feet at all,
and weeping.

It was natural enough that this strange thing
should be talked about in a village where the
people were so settled in their foolishness as to
believe in the real existence of fire-drakes and
Nellie-birds.

This sadness of the fisherman could well
have been attributed to the rude way the children treated him, for whenever a chance
occurred they would rush out upon him and
upset his basket of fish, that he was perhaps
carrying to the vicarage, into the dust of the
road.

Had the fisherman brought sorrow or glad-
ness to Mockery? This was a point that the
dwellers in the little Gap answered differently.

Mrs. Topple said nothing; but Mr. Cheney
wasn't sorry now that he had come, because the
excitement prevented any one from noticing

that he had dug a tunnel into the centre of the tumulus upon the cliff, hoping to find the golden earrings.

. . .

Mr. Pattimore now stood—feeling the queer sensation of one who holds in his hand something that has been hidden for many a long year—beside his garden hedge, with his kite, that possessed a fine tail, ten yards in length.

He wanted the rude children; he wanted to get them back to better manners, as became their Bible names, by means of his kite.

But where were the rude children? Mr. Pattimore could see no one.

But no, he was wrong, for some one was passing.

This passer-by was Mrs. Pring, who walked a little and then waited and looked about her as though something queer had happened in the village and she wished to discover what it was.

Mrs. Pattimore, after speaking to Miss Pink, who was merely going to her cottage from the shop, had naturally followed her husband's footsteps and was gone into the bedroom after he had left it in order to tidy the wardrobe, that she knew he would leave in confusion.

Mr. Pattimore looked about for the children, but only saw Mrs. Pring.

At the further corner of the vicarage garden there was a small gate, intended perhaps by the designer of the garden to provide a poor clergyman a way of escape from the tax-gatherer, or the village beggar man. To this gate, that was but a few yards from Mrs. Pottle's cottage, Mr. Pattimore betook him-self, still carrying his great kite. And from there he watched an event that certainly as-tonished him in no small degree, considering how he as well as every one else in Mockery knew all about the quarrel between the Prings and the Pottles.

As a rule, Mrs. Pring would pass by Mrs. Pottle's cottage with her eyes more than half closed and with the look of a woman who hates her neighbour most heartily. She would even stand for a moment and listen and then, hearing the tick of a clock, she would shake her head and mutter between her teeth, ''Tis only a very common clock that be going.'

Whether Mr. Pattimore fancied at that moment that the children had flown up into the sky, we do not know, but he looked up, perhaps to notice, in the interest of his kite flying, whether the winds were blowing.

Above him there happened to be settled a large black cloud like a great bird. Looking down from the cloud again, Mr. Pattimore beheld Mrs. Pring go near to Mrs. Pottle, who was standing in her garden, and speak to her.

'What be the right time?' inquired Mrs. Pring. Mr. Pattimore stared in astonishment.

Mrs. Pottle went into the house; she returned therefrom proudly, and replied that it was four o'clock.

'Mary Gulliver, her that be called t' other Mary in village'—Mrs. Pring was now talking as though to an intimate friend—'she be got like it.'

Mr. Pattimore couldn't run away. To make any movement would be to betray that he was there, and that he was listening, and so he remained very still.

'Mr. Gulliver,' said Mrs. Pottle, taking from the hedge the very garment that Mr. Pattimore had tried to see instead of the muslin frock, ''e that do believe in monsters, be a strict father to 'is maid.'

'If anything were to happen, 'e 'd as soon turn she into road as spit into fire.'

'Yes, and though a man mid allow all the rabbits in Mockery to live rent-free in 's meadow lands, same as 'e do live 'isself—'e may be funny.'

''E be funny,' said Mrs. Pring. 'If she's baby do come, without she being a wife, 'twill be murder.'

Mrs. Pottle looked gloomily at the sky. 'Where be all they children gone?' she inquired.

Mrs. Pring opened the cottage gate and went nearer still to Mrs. Pottle.

''Tis thik fisherman,' she said, 'that all be

following, except they who bain't willing to leave their homes.'

'Ducks do swim upon Mr. Caddy's pond, and 'e bain't there.'

'Wold Pring be gone.'

'Mrs. Cheney do follow where her son Simon do go.'

'Wold Cheney do bide home.'

'Or else do dig on hill for gold.'

'But Mrs. Topple don't notice nothing, only they leaves.'

'Mother Moggs don't leave her shop where white mice do bide.'

'All they maids be gone.'

'Children be gone.'

The cloud hung silent.

'Where be Mrs. Pattimore?' asked Mrs. Pring.

'She be gone after fisherman too,' answered Mrs. Pottle.

A gust of wind that is named in Norfolk a Rogers blast came upon Mr. Pattimore with all the suddenness of an explosion, and carried —as if it were come for that very purpose—the kite away.

The women saw it go, and, taking the same fright that hens do when they see a hawk above, hurried both together into Mrs. Pottle's doorway, exclaiming that the Nellie-bird was come to destroy them all.

The cloud, as soon as it had brought the

blast that carried off Mr. Pattimore's kite, immediately disappeared, and the sun shone and a fresh summer wind blew that took the kite higher. The ball of string to which the kite was attached had unwound rapidly, though the end still remained in Mr. Pattimore's hand.

Mr. Pattimore now felt that he was being strangely guided in a manner that Dean Ashbourne could never have expected and so had never advised him about. The string tugged at him, as the kite, borne aloft by a pretty strong breeze from the north, sailed over the Mockery meadows.

Mr. Pattimore clambered through the hedge and so followed the kite, but the string with an extra jerk slipped through his hand and was gone.

The kite as soon as ever it felt itself free went along in fine fashion, until the string managed to become entangled in one of the trees of Mockery wood, and the kite remained almost stationary in the sky.

Mr. Pattimore saw it there, and, bethinking himself of the star that led the wise men of the East, he followed to the wood.

In the centre of Mockery wood there used to be—at least when the writer of this tale first trespassed there—a ruined church. This church—and it was certainly still there when Mr. Pattimore lived in Mockery—was very much hidden. Those visitors, Mr. James

Tarr, Miss Ogle, and the rest, hadn't found it; indeed, few people—even in this day when everything is discovered, except the peace of God (that none wish for)—know that if they trespass far into Mockery wood they will find a church.

When he crossed the meadow in order to reach the wood, above which the kite merrily floated in the summer airs, Mr. Pattimore came upon another person—he passed Mr. Pring returning to the village again—who was watching the kite too. This was Mrs. Topple, who while looking in the lanes for clover had seen the kite go by, and had followed it for nearly the same reason as Mr. Pattimore, only instead of a truant wife it was a fine stalk of clover that she hoped it would lead her to.

Mrs. Topple appeared to be careworn and haggard; her white face looked down, as if all the hope of finding what she wished for had long ago fled away, and now she had nothing to do but to look down at the ground for ever and until the end.

But Mrs. Topple wasn't the only one who had wandered out that evening of strange happenings. For, going down into a little hollow in the field where a pit used to be, Mr. Pattimore came upon the smallholder Gulliver, who was staring up at the kite in a wild manner, and who at once, as soon as he saw the clergyman, began to declare that a flying fish must have broken loose from India: 'And 'tis most likely,' said Mr. Gulliver, 'that the Caribs will follow, who do eat men, and 'tain't likely they will miss over me poor Mary, who be plump and tasty.'

'Where is the other Mary, then?' asked Mr. Pattimore, catching, though most unaccountably, the fears of Gulliver.

'She be gone down to the sea, where Caribs do come from,' was the mournful reply. And Mr. Gulliver, evidently seeing all the other Mary as devoured beyond recall, walked sadly across the meadow in the direction of his home.

The evening, though fair on the whole, was behaving as if it wished to hasten the coming midsummer night by allowing dark clouds to hang in the sky and to remain still—for no wind blasts came now—above Mockery Gap.

As Mr. Pattimore entered the wood, the dimness caused by the clouds and the leafy trees so darkened his path that he feared it wouldn't be easy to find the tree that flew his kite.

Mr. Pattimore was uncertain which way to go.

The scent of a wood, heavy-laden with all summer growings, carried Mr. Pattimore back to his childhood as the kite had done. In just such a wood had he and his little sister played at being the Babes, until his father, who appeared at the very moment when the children were covering themselves with leaves, discovered them and sent them to bed.

The trees in Mockery wood—and Mr. Pink had never been able to do anything about them —had an uncomfortable habit of falling over each other that made wandering under their shadows a little tiresome. But this habit suited some people, for to Miss Dinah Pottle's satisfaction there were always plenty of fallen boughs, and Mr. Caddy was always perfectly right when he said 'that soft beds abounded everywhere in Mockery wood.'

Sometimes before we know it new surroundings will make us strange to ourselves and do odd things.

Near to the portrait of the Dean, Mr. Pattimore had been up to that moment, if we except the honeymoon, only mindful that he abode with a Dorcas in all humbleness and chastity. But now, in the silence of the wood and with no one near to him but a white owl that sat and winked above its hole in a hollow tree, Mr. Pattimore spoke softly the word 'Nellie.'

Mr. Pattimore slowly made his way along deeper into the wood, where denser weeds grew and where the fallen trees more than ever encumbered the way.

He went by the place, a fair mossy bank, where Mr. Gulliver, having peeped into the wood—for no other or better reason than to see what a wood looked like—beheld the monster.

The scent of the wood weeds grew sweeter. Mr. Pattimore forgot the kite, he almost forgot himself—he listened. A sound of merriment, the call of happy voices, and a song that went with a children's dance came to him from somewhere in the wood. These sounds ceased soon, as sounds will that are so doubtfully heard as scarcely to be believed in. But soon again, and quite near to him this time, Mr. Pattimore heard sounds—voices.

He broke through a few low bushes and listened.

Some one was there, and quite near by. 'Even though thee bain't nor duck,' a voice said, 'thee mid be better to listen than wold owl in tree that I've been talking to.'

'I came here to look for my husband, who's lost his kite,' a soft voice said.

''Twasn't nor kite,' said the other in an annoyed tone. ''Twas thik Nellie-bird.'

Mr. Pattimore clambered on. 'Nellie,' he said, 'Nellie.'

He hardly knew what he said, but at the next step he made he slipped and fell, spraining his ankle. He tried to stand, but the pain was too much and he fell again. He crawled a little, hoping to hear the voices again. But he heard nothing. He was now near to a glade that continued, though Mr. Pattimore did not know it, all the length of the wood and at last reached the sea.

Mr. Pattimore had climbed a little grassy bank, and the glade was below him.

He groaned because of the pain that he was in, and waited; the evening was full of strange sounds.

The singing had begun again, the dance song. A little higher up the glade, where the ruined church was, the singing sounded more and more clearly.

At last, from an old archway that Mr. Pattimore could but dimly see, a group of merry children came dancing; each child carried a foxglove in its hand, and was singing.

They passed by Mr. Pattimore.

Behind the children came the new fisherman, and with him, holding his hand, was Esther. And soon Rebecca and Dinah and Mary passed silently behind them.

They were not gone out of sight before two more, a couple in close conversation, came by— Mrs. Pattimore and Mr. Caddy.

Mr. Pattimore shut his eyes.

When he opened them, he wondered what he had better do in order to get out of the wood.

He decided to crawl, and had proceeded, indeed, for a little way, until he encountered— for this summer evening was indeed an exceptional one—a god in distress.

For upon the mossy stump where the hermit of old was wont to pray, Mr. Pattimore found Simon Cheney.

This young gentleman was lying upon his face, and, after the usual custom of little gods when they don't get exactly what they want, he was screaming and kicking with vexation and grief.

Mrs. Cheney leant over her son, sobbing too.

Simon sat up.

'They be all after thik b . . . fisherman,' he said fiercely. 'There bain't no maiden for I these days; 'tis to fisherman they do go.'

'And me son Simon did only follow the Nellie-bird,' groaned Mrs. Cheney.

'And did climb tree, and did only bring down a blasted wold kite,' moaned the god.

Mr. Pattimore now saw his kite, that was lying in shreds at his feet, having been destroyed by the anger of the god when the three maids in the wood refused to allow him to go with them.

Mr. Pattimore tried to rise; he wished to tell God Simon that if he would only listen to Dean Ashbourne he would need no maidens to solace him in woods or fields.

In trying to rise he gave his foot a twist and hurt it more than ever.

Mr. Pattimore fainted.

Chapter 25

THE LOVE MESSAGE

ALTHOUGH death often leaves old women alone for a long time, he sometimes pounces upon them two or three at a time and takes them off with him.

Old women, and especially those who have little or no money—Miss Pink, since the strange disappearance of her brother, lived upon the charity of a good Roddy, who, although he collected stones, had a heart of flesh—are not always unwilling to die. But there are some old women who don't want to go.

Earlier in the summer, Mr. Caddy, though this must have cost him an effort, left the bed out of the story when he happened to meet Mrs. Pring by the church gate, and merely told her that the doctor had been to see Miss Pink, and had put on his gloves slowly and had shaken his head before he started his car that he always drove so carefully.

''E don't shake 'is head for nothing,' said Mr. Caddy.

'Were she in front room or upstairs?' inquired Mrs. Pring, expecting the usual word from Mr. Caddy.

Mr. Caddy looked at a gravestone and never replied.

In Mockery every one notices which way a

person takes who leaves a cottage to go for a little walk.

Up till the day of the doctor's visit, Miss Pink would usually take the lane that went by the churchyard, and going a few hundred yards further she would turn when she reached Farmer Cheney's old barn and come home by the same way.

But now she always went in the opposite direction.

Besides this sign of a certain difference in Miss Pink's ways, she had begun to do something else a little while after her brother went, that the people of Mockery couldn't in the least understand.

For Miss Pink had taken to visiting her poorer neighbours.

When a morning knock was heard at any cottage door, there would be Miss Pink with her large shawl, her little nose looking smaller than ever, and her eyes looking afraid—'as if,' Mrs. Pottle said, 'something nasty were running after she.'

Miss Pink would, of course, be shown into the front room, and would take the best chair, and sigh heavily, and look up at the clock —when she called at Mrs. Pottle's—without speaking. She would stay looking for half an hour, and then go out into the lane again.

Mr. Caddy couldn't help—seeing how

things were with Miss Pink—making a remark
or two to his ducks about her.

"Twill be t' other turning for she soon,'
Mr. Caddy would say, nodding to the ducks
in the pond, whenever Miss Pink came out of
her cottage and went up the lane.

'An' bed thik wold maid be a-going to be
a silent one.'

Miss Pink was now worse; indeed, her pain
rarely left her. But she still kept her front
room as tidy as she could, and waited for her
expected visitor.

Summer weather, though our joys are
heightened by the clear and plenteous shining
of the sun, cannot lift the dark shadow of the
cloud of death when it is near; but rather the
summer darkens the horror by the very beauty
of its shining.

The beast—Miss Pink had known for some
while now what he was—horned and fearful,
was coming up out of the sea to take her away.

But now she was smiling; this wasn't because her pain had stopped for a moment, but
merely because her front room, the morning
after the children had come out of the Mockery
wood singing, looked so neat and tidy, and
Miss Pink felt sure that if ever she were going
to receive an answer to her letter she would
receive it now.

And there—for Miss Pink had peeped out
of the window—was Mr. Pring, that faithful

messenger, picking up a piece of paper in the road.

A message from—no, not from Mr. Gulliver; she had long given him up—but from some other one who wanted her at His wedding.

Miss Pink's heart beat fast; she watched Mr. Pring.

He took an envelope out of his trousers pocket, looked at it, and put it back into his pocket again.

He then folded the paper that he had picked up, and walked slowly and thoughtfully towards Miss Pink's cottage, muttering to himself.

Miss Pink waited, waited in excited expectation for her letter—was he bringing it to her? Yes, Mr. Pring was even then murmuring words by her little gate: 'Pring be the one to carry a message; wold Pring don't never lose a letter.' The next thing he did was to drop the folded paper with careful deliberation into the road again, and go back to his work still muttering how good he was at carrying a letter.

'It's my letter,' said Miss Pink; 'my brother always said I would have it one day.'

Her pain came again; it had only left her for a moment so as to gather strength for a new attack. And now it came and told her that the beast was very near.

Miss Pink stepped from her gate, found the

paper, and read the message. It was merely a page that had fluttered from Mr. Pattimore's Bible on his way to church. Some words were underlined. Miss Pink read them: 'Behold, the bridegroom cometh; go ye out to meet him.'

And Miss Pink went out into the Mockery lanes to find her lover.

Chapter 26

SILENT BELLS

Miss Pink waited in the lanes; she felt unable to find her lover unless some one, other than the summer day, guided her to Him. Who this might be Miss Pink did not know, but she waited.

Miss Pink waited, and looked towards Mrs. Moggs' shop.

Mrs. Moggs had awakened that morning very hopeful and happy. The evening before, for some reason or other, the Mockery children hadn't come in to worry her, and also she felt sure that when she came downstairs and peeped into a certain drawer she would find little baby mice.

But these were not the only reasons why Mrs. Moggs was more than usually happy that day. There was another, and that was, that the town postmaster, Mr. Hunt, had apparently forgotten the village.

'Perhaps,' thought Mrs. Moggs, ringing her bells, and showing in her thought the innocence of her nature—'perhaps he will never come again.'

Mrs. Moggs had dressed herself slowly, and stood for a while before her glass to make her bells ring.

When she was downstairs and looked into the drawer to see how many mice were born, she counted five. She was so glad to see them that she hardly noticed that the mice had bitten a hole into the other drawer where the stamps and postal orders were kept. But when she wiped her glasses and looked more closely at the nest she saw that it was made up of little coloured bits of paper.

Mrs. Moggs trembled. She had only a moment before looked out of the window and seen Miss Pink standing in the lane; and now a large motor car was drawn up at her door, and a man was stepping out of it.

Mrs. Moggs turned very pale as Mr. Hunt in his noisiest manner came into the shop and at once demanded of her an exact account of the stamps and orders that she had sold.

While Mrs. Moggs looked for her books, Esther Pottle opened the door and, holding out some pence in her hand, said: 'These are for the stamps that mother owes you for.'

Mr. Hunt looked so fiercely at Esther that she dropped all her pennies.

'Yes, I see,' said Mr. Hunt, who had glanced at the figures; 'and now bring to me all the orders that you have in stock, please.'

'But where are the rest of them?' asked Mr. Hunt, after counting carefully all that Mrs. Moggs brought to him.

'The mice,' said Mrs. Moggs, trembling, 'the white mice.'

'You're a liar!' shouted Mr. Hunt.

Mrs. Moggs couldn't see Mr. Hunt now, but she knew that from somewhere or other, perhaps from those islands that he had gone to, Mr. Pink was telling her about the beautiful sea. The shop faded too, and Mr. Hunt went as a bad dream goes, while before her she saw the beautiful sea—only the sea.

Mr. Hunt was gone, and Esther picked up the pennies and laid them upon the counter.

Mrs. Moggs fetched her bonnet and cloak. In the lane she met Miss Pink, who appeared to have been waiting for her.

'I am going to the beautiful sea,' said Mrs. Moggs, nodding her head, while her bells rang merrily.

'And I will go with you,' said Miss Pink.

Miss Pink helped Mrs. Moggs over the stile; they walked in the meadows together.

Since she had received her letter, Miss Pink saw all her life as pointing one way—to her lover. Mr. Gulliver who had not replied to her, her brother leaving her with no word, her illness and her ever-recurring pain—all this trouble she felt was soon to be completed and soon to be changed to joy. She was aware, however, that perhaps her lover might wish her to do some kind last act; to love an enemy, an enemy whom she had always dreaded, before he took her to Himself.

Miss Pink had never dared to go and look at the sea ever since Mr. Tarr had told her that the beast would come out of it. But now, having had her letter, she cared not what she saw, and she even felt brave enough to save the beast from drowning if such a strange chance occurred. Suppose she were to see the beast trying to get up out of the sea, she would now even dare to help it. Miss Pink felt as she walked that she should have been kinder in her thoughts to the horrid creature.

'What have I done,' said Miss Pink, thinking her thoughts aloud, 'to help or save any one? When I have seen Mrs. Pottle beating her kittens to death and calling them Prings, that she used to do every time the poor cat had its family, I never laid down in the path and told her to beat me instead and to call me Mrs. Pring. And when I once saw Simon Cheney treating poor Dinah cruelly and in a very wicked way, I never offered to allow him to do his worst with me instead.'

'We are going to the beautiful sea,' said Mrs. Moggs, interrupting Miss Pink's thoughts.

The two women walked down to the beach together; they held each other by the hand. They stepped cautiously over the shining pebbles that were warmed in the sun.

The sea was very still; during all the time that poor Mr. Dobbin had lived there it had never once been so still. In the distance there was a haze that comes only upon a sultry summer's day. But the tide was very high.

'So this is the beautiful sea,' said Mrs. Moggs a little disappointedly.

When there was a high tide the sea almost covered the Blind Cow Rock. A small portion of the rock was now only just above the water.

Miss Pink uttered a cry of fear.

Upon the rock that now and again a little gentle wave would wash, there was standing in an attitude of extreme distress Mr. Dobbin's monkey.

'It's the dreadful beast,' said Miss Pink, and shuddered.

Mrs. Moggs looked at the beast too, and then at her carefully blacked Sunday shoes, that seemed to have led her to a very strange church that day, and all because she wanted so much to escape from the horrid words of Mr. Hunt the postmaster.

'It's the dreadful beast that Mr. Tarr spoke of, though it hasn't the horns,' said Miss Pink in a voice of terror; 'and he's coming to drown us all.'

'He looks very unhappy,' remarked Mrs. Moggs, 'and I think he is afraid of being drowned himself.'

The tide was still rising.

Certain words that Miss Pink remembered reading somewhere—words spoken by the grand Lover of mankind—came into her mind: 'But I say unto you, Love your enemies, bless them that curse you——'

'I will save the poor beast from drowning,' said Miss Pink, and without a thought as to what might happen to herself she stepped into the sea. She sank at once like a stone. Mrs. Moggs looked for the monkey; he was gone too.

In a few moments Mrs. Moggs saw Miss Pink's shawl floating upon the water. 'Miss Pink must be under her shawl,' said Mrs. Moggs, 'and I mustn't go home and leave her in the beautiful sea.'

Mrs. Moggs regarded Miss Pink's shawl thoughtfully; she looked down at her own shoes: so far she had not wetted them.

'Mr. Caddy says,' remarked Mrs. Moggs, looking into the sea, as if she expected Miss Pink to hear what she said, 'that the sea never likes old women enough to want to hurt them. He says 'tis the young girls the waves be after. Miss Pink,' said Mrs. Moggs loudly, 'don't go too far down.'

Mrs. Moggs stepped into the sea.

An hour later, when the fisherman was passing, he found Paul's body washed up by the sea. He buried him deeply in the sands.

Chapter 27

MRS. TOPPLE GOES TO HEAVEN

MR. CADDY, when he advised Mrs. Topple to look for clover in the road, had an even kinder thought for her than had Mr. Tarr when he advised her in the interest of healing all her pains to hunt for the magic leaf.

Mr. Caddy had grown thoughtful and silent when Mr. Hunt—who never even came back to say he was sorry for what he had done—rode over his best duck and deprived her of life. It was then, in the innocence of Mr. Caddy's heart, who fancied that the wicked are sometimes punished, that he decided that could Mr. Hunt be persuaded to drive over a human being he might get hanged for it.

When a child, Mr. Caddy had known the Maidenbridge hangman and had liked him.

"'Twouldn't hurt poor Mrs. Topple to die all of a sudden,' Mr. Caddy had wisely informed his friends in the pond, 'for 'tain't here upon earth that she mid find thik fine clover; 'tis in they golden fields of heaven.'

With this praiseworthy desire to get Mrs. Topple, as soon as convenient to the angels, to the upper meadows where all the clover has four leaves, he advised the lady to look in the road for what she wanted, knowing how fast Mr. Hunt drove his car round the worst corners.

If any one person in the Mockery world was believed by all, that person was Mr. Caddy. For he who knows all the ins and outs of everything, all the bedtime manners, all the happy courting in the woods and meadows, all the many and merry ways of country matters that are used in the shaping of a man—how could such a one be ever doubted when he gave advice?

Mrs. Topple believed that Mr. Caddy had pointed out to her, as he had done to so many a Mockery maiden, the way to be happy, and so as soon as the holidays were come she began to hunt in the lanes as he had advised her to do. And she had just knelt beside a bank that had itself crept a little too far into the road for safety, to pick the very thing that she had searched so diligently for all that warm summer, a four-leaf clover, when Mr. Hunt, who was in a hurry to send the Dodder policeman after Mrs. Moggs—for ever since he had seen her happy curls he had wished her in prison—ran into her.

Mr. Hunt's car was a heavy one, and the bonnet struck Mrs. Topple's head, and took from her all thought of her happiness by rendering her utterly unconscious of anything at all.

Mr. Hunt rushed on, and soon discovered the Dodder policeman, who was talking to a girl in the road, and sent him off to Mockery to arrest Mrs. Moggs, and also to look to a woman who had had a seizure in the lane, after falling down a high bank, to the immediate danger of any poor motorist who might want to pass.

The policeman found Mrs. Topple dead with the clover in her hand.

Chapter 28

STRANGE FISH

MR. GULLIVER had never seen any one casting a net, and so, when he released his cows from the narrow lane into the wide meadow that was next to the sea, he thought he would go down this summer afternoon and watch the fisherman, who was then casting out from his boat a net into the sea.

The Mockery children, who were oddly quiet now, were watching too, and Simon Cheney might have been there had he wished, but he had gone to Mr. Gulliver's cottage hoping that Mary would let him in, now that her father was out of the way.

Mr. Gulliver stood a little apart from the waves, upon the edge of his own field, where a few rushes grew.

He was thoughtful, though he did not think at the moment about his monsters; but wondered, as many a simple-minded father has wondered before him, why the other Mary had lost her happy colour and was become so pensive and so sad.

'She used to dance and run,' he thought, 'but now she do walk slow.'

A wise parent often shuts his eyes tight to what is happening, and thus, although Mr. Gulliver was always willing enough to listen, he never looked. But the other Mockery eyes were open enough though his were shut, and, with the exception perhaps of Mrs. Pattimore, all knew what Mary's trouble was, and why she looked so pale.

'A pretty maid,' Mr. Caddy had often told those wise ducks of his, who were the best of listeners, 'don't lie down upon they green bank beds for nothing, when Simon Peter be about.'

And often when Mary went by the pond, wearing an apron over her thin summer frock, she would look longingly at Mr. Caddy's ducks as if to ask for their advice in her trouble.

Every one wonders, and very naturally too, what would happen if a boy let off a water pistol in the face of a dean—Dean Ashbourne, most likely, as he was standing—such a stern one!—in his cathedral pew. And this same sort of wonder was running in Mockery as to how Mr. Gulliver would take an event that must be very soon.

Mr. Gulliver, though very kind to rabbits and very interested in monsters, was, as we know, one of those who believed entirely in a very strict set of proper manners in a home, having never forgotten Mr. Pattimore's precepts delivered to him after his wife was buried.

'Never,' he used to say to Mary, when she would tell him how naughty the sky looked and how naked the earth, while Simon always had clothes about him, and she too—'never has one of they babies come to our home before the maid be married.'

No one, and certainly not Mary, 'she that be t' other,' as the rude children had called her, could bear to think for a moment of anything that came naked into the world. Such a happening must point from everlasting to a dire state of iniquity, for born nakedly showed backwards as well as forwards an awful wickedness.

And so Mary, with a secret fear in her heart that one day she might behold something as shameful as the sky when it is reddest, went her ways a little sadly, and sat at home sometimes while Mr. Gulliver drove out the cows to the meadows, wishing, no doubt, that God Simon might knock at her door with the wedding-ring.

Ever since the arrival of the Nellie-bird—for all the village called him that now—the Mockery sea had altered its complexion in the eyes of the Mockery folk.

For one thing, some who had never been near to it, such as Mrs. Moggs, and others too, now came to look, if not wholly to taste of the waters.

Before the arrival of the Nellie-bird, the people had regarded the sea as an odd sort of person, a little like Mr. Pring's weather, though whether beast, man, or woman they could never determine. Certainly they were sure that the sea was silly, if not gone entirely foolish in the head, having formed the ridiculous habit of foaming with its many mouths open and distorting its features into the most ugly grimaces.

'They jumping waters bain't got all their senses,' Mrs. Pring had once informed Mr. Gulliver. And even poor unnoticed John Pottle, a character that the wise Wang might have written of, did notice as he carried Dinah's faggot—not out of politeness, but only to hide himself the more—that the sea had departed, in a sulky fit of springtime madness, almost entirely out of sight.

Besides looking so foolish, Mockery was well aware that the sea also showed the uneasiness of its habits by casting up—'sicking up,' Mrs. Pottle would have said—all sorts of things in such a variety that a small basket of them would have provided Mr. James Tarr with all the matter he needed for a lecture of some hours.

There was the monkey, and the torpedo, and the dead nigger that the former fisherman, Mr. Dobbin, came upon and wished himself anywhere else but on the seashore when he made the last discovery.

Besides much else, there was the sealed bottle that Mr. Pink had found, that contained a little slip of paper, upon which was written in a classical hand, 'Beware of the horned beast.'

If any one had ever seen the sea in a concrete manner it might have been Mrs. Pring, who thought one day, looking at the waves from her garden, that the sea was like an old bull with a white curly head, having the same restless habits and manners as Mr. Cheney's when he played with the cows.

The tides were always a mystery. For honest John had reported to Mr. Caddy, who was very much frightened at the time for fear that his pond might behave in the same manner, that 'there bain't nor sea.'

On the other hand, when the waves were right up to the wood one day, and Mother Pottle was helping Dinah with her sticks, that lady supposed that the earth had one night been cut through at that point by the devil, and that God, in order to hold the earth together again, had filled up the gap with salt water instead of glue.

In any country place, when two or three are gathered together, something of interest is always expected to happen. Boors and stablemen, cottage women and shadows, will often stand near to one another in the fond hope that something may come of it; and if only a rat run out from between the stones of Farmer Cheney's barn, or a slut of a girl run by, raising her skirts naughtily at the men, the company return to their homes and feel that something has been done.

The Mockery children, tamer now and more silent, are watching the fisherman, hoping to get again the same sort of excitement that they had in the wood. Esther is with them, and they do not even stone her, though there are plenty of stones; and Dinah too, who has no trouble—though she certainly, as well as Rebecca, deserved to have—can cheerfully be with the children and watch the Nellie-bird.

Those who have never been near to the sea, except when by chance the sea has been near to them, are near to it now. Mrs. Pottle and Mrs. Pring, with their shadows lying together upon the sands, are at the very sea's edge, and regard the waters with true human greed, hoping to have the first chance to steal a mackerel, supposing the fisherman do catch any.

Although the waters were not home, Mrs. Pottle looked at them exactly as though they were the fine clock upon her mantel that could tick so loudly.

The waves splashed, and the same thoughts were in her mind about them as when the clock ticked, for the sea was there to yield up its mackerel to her as the clock its minutes.

Mrs Pring looked not only into the water, but sometimes at the rough blackness of the Blind Cow Rock, in the pleased manner of one who has a better cow at home than her neighbour has.

'Poor Mrs. Topple,' remarked Mrs. Pottle, eyeing the movements of the fisherman, who was now getting his net in nearer to the shore; 'she were so glad to find leaf, that Mr. Tarr did tell of, that she did fall down from high bank to strike they rough stones in lane.'

'And policeman did say "natural causes" before 'e turned she over in road.'

'And true 'twere a natural cause for teacher to want to heal they pains in she's leg.'

'We do all want to get well.'

'So we do,' said Mrs. Pottle.

'Children do stay quiet,' murmured Mrs. Pring.

'But now they bain't so noisy they be more hungry, and Esther, now that she don't run out to be naughty in lane, be always asking for fish for dinner.'

''Tis to be hoped that fisherman do catch a mackerel; but see, they children be going to help fisherman.'

Besides the two women, who were watching with astonishment the children standing near the fisherman and pulling in the net, Mr. Pring and Mr. Gulliver were watching with wonder too, for neither of them had ever seen the Mockery children perform any act other than a naughty one.

The women moved nearer.

The holy peace of a summer's afternoon, sweet as the scent of the lily-of-the-valley,

visited the scene. The green shade of the wood
darkened the colour of the sea, while the sea,
with its tiny waves warmed, happily danced.
But the Blind Cow Rock cast a black shadow.

The women watched, holding out their
hands. They expected at any moment to see
the splash of the shining bodies of the fish.

But the fisherman, although the sun shone
upon his hair and beard, his cap being cast to
one side, didn't look so free and gay as usual.
He wasn't singing, his happy manners were
changed to his sad ones, so that Mrs. Pring
fancied that she could recognise in him even a
look of the unfortunate Mr. Dobbin.

The afternoon's catch was certainly very
near to the shore now; but whatever it was
that the fisherman had in his net—and it
appeared very heavy—he didn't wish the children to stay close by. Perhaps he supposed
that their former ways would return and that
they would bite and scratch one another to get
hold of the fishes.

He even told Esther and Dinah to go away
too, though Esther considered herself now to
be every bit as grown-up as her cousin, and as
well able to love anything or to see anything
as ever was Dinah when Simon followed her
into the wood.

The children went, as the fisherman told
them to do, into the wood to gather sticks, and
Esther and Dinah walked slowly along the lane

to their cottage, chattering about different coloured ribbons, and much disappointed that they were not allowed to see the fish that the Nellie-bird had caught in his net.

But in the place of the children a new helper had arrived. This was Mr. Caddy, who had informed his ducks that he had two good reasons for going down to the sea this afternoon. One was that his wife was washing, an occupation to which he hated to be anywhere near, because once—and this happened the very day that Mr. Tarr descended upon the village—Mrs. Caddy had asked her husband to wring a blanket.

''Twas a suggestion,' Mr. Caddy told the ducks, 'that I don't wish to hear never again.'

And so as a rule when the copper was heating Mr. Caddy would walk away.

The second reason was—and a simple one— that Mr. Caddy, since Pottle had told him it wasn't anywhere, had a natural desire to note if the sea had come back again.

And now Mr. Caddy, finding that the sea was come, looked into it most uncomfortably, because the fisherman invited him to help with the net.

Mr. Caddy decided that the sea had betrayed him, and that in future he would take the way to the churchyard, where the folk didn't pull at nets or wash clothes, but lay always happy in wormy beds—Caddy's own favourite word—like logs of wood who possessed better manners than to become coal.

The catch was now brought in and laid upon the warmed sand.

"'Tain't no monster, be en, 'tain't no tiger?' inquired Mr. Gulliver, coming down slowly to the sands, to which Mr. Pring had descended before him.

'No,' replied Mr. Pring, 'nor a bear neither. . . .'

Mr. Caddy bent down pityingly over the two drowned women, who were holding one another. He covered their faces with Miss Pink's shawl that had been caught in the net too and brought to shore.

'They bells be silent now,' said Mr. Caddy, 'and Miss Pink's nose be hid for ever.'

'So it be,' remarked Mr. Pring.

'An' Mother Moggs won't be called a liar no more.'

As he followed Mr. Gulliver's waggon, in which the sad burdens netted in the sea were placed tenderly, Mr. Caddy bethought him of his ducks and of the story he would have to tell them of his first and last visit to the Mockery sea.

Chapter 29

THE OTHER MARY

I⊤ was the first Sunday in September, and the first cool wind from the north blew over Mockery Gap, as if to remind any one who wished to play while the summer lingered to hurry to the meadows.

Mr. Pattimore now felt safer and more protected against that snare to the flesh, poor Dorcas, than he had been for some weeks.

He had been laid up, chastised by God—possibly by means of a prayer from Dean Ashbourne—with a sprained ankle, in the upper chamber.

Evidently this chastisement had come because he had said more than once, with the same kind of wanton thoughts that had met him in the wood, the name 'Nellie.'

All the while he was in bed—and he was there until he knew each lump in his mattress as if it was his nearest relation—she was 'Dorcas,' and when he went out again she was 'Dorcas' still.

'I mustn't,' he said, when he was downstairs once more, 'ever look at the sea, for it was there too, when I caught those fish with the fisherman, that former things came into my mind.'

During his first walk, that he took with the help of a stick, he had boldly confronted the fisherman, who was dancing with the children upon the green, while Mr. Pottle, noticed at last because he could play the flute, provided the music.

Mr. Pattimore spoke strongly; he told the fisherman that he ought to be catching cod-fish far out in the wide waters of the ocean, instead of playing with the children and allowing himself to be called the Nellie-bird, a name that could be found nowhere in the Bible.

'You have only,' said Mr. Pattimore, 'shown the children a new way to be wicked; for now, instead of shouting out bad words and stoning the cats, they play games with singing and dance to damnation.'

This walk was upon a Saturday, and now that Sunday was come Mr. Pattimore preached from a favourite text—a little altered to taste—that a dean must be blameless.

His high hopes, however, of becoming one had, ever since the new fisherman had come to Mockery, been but futile.

During all this time Dean Ashbourne had written but one postcard to 'Dorcas,' to inform her that he was going to marry his third wife. (Let us say at once for the credit of the Church that the other two were really dead, and that the new one, a blooming young person of five-and-twenty, was very much alive.)

'He's getting quite a David,' said Dorcas, helping her husband to a little bacon.

Mr. Pattimore didn't answer.

Later, in church, Dorcas sat meek in her pew, and when she knelt down she pressed her red lips against her hand and thought of her husband, and how he was so merry and queer five years ago in the hollow of the cliff. She hid a blush in her Prayer-book, and wondered if any one had seen.

Beside Mrs. Pattimore, Mary Gulliver had also accepted one of the one hundred and eighty-two sittings. She had bought a new coat, a long one that hid her shape, telling her father, as an excuse for buying it, that the new woman at the shop, Mrs. Gentle, had said she found the church very draughty; 'and I do too,' said Mary.

Mr. Pattimore looked hard at Mary when he preached, and he stopped for a moment in order to put more force into his words when they came, and he told her to 'beware of all nakedness.'

God Simon was standing beside the church gate, when Mary went out into the lane, with two girl companions, imported, with the promise of many presents, from Dodder.

They were standing under an elm, the pro-truding roots of which looked like large elephants' heads.

Simon and the girls stared hard at Mary and laughed loudly.

As a general rule, Mary walked out with

Rebecca and Dinah upon Sunday afternoons. She would call at Dinah's cottage, and together they would fetch Rebecca from the vicarage, and sometimes Esther would go with them. But this Sunday evening Mary walked alone in the lower meadows of Mockery.

Mary had very much admired, when she read it the day before, all that had been said in the *Western Times* about the sad end of Miss Pink and Mrs. Moggs.

"'Twould be a nice bit,' thought Mary, feeling her trouble at that moment remind her of its presence, 'that would be said about I; an' London river be full up of poor girls.'

Mary had read something of this kind in the paper, referring to the pleasure that London girls took in ending their lives in the river. And as Mary had never seen a river, she thought the Thames at London to be something like Mr. Caddy's pond, only larger, and containing pretty water-weeds to lie back upon when one is tired of one's trouble.

As soon as ever the girls at the church gate had laughed, Mary decided to do as the other ones did so often. She knew her father, and she shared with him a proper abhorrence of the arrival of anything so like the red naked sky as a baby, unless one is conventionally clothed in the garment of marriage. She couldn't bear to think how her father, after listening to her through all the summer telling the amusing stories about Simon's manners on the hill, should now have forced upon him the nakedness of reality; a natural order in life, perhaps, but one that the good farmer, and we think rightly, detested manfully.

When the other Mary reached the sands with intent to destroy herself in the sea, she couldn't help bending down to reach a little shell that she admired, and wondering a little, as she looked at it, at the strong determination in her heart that had brought her down to the shore that day.

This determination took her along with a firm step until she stood opposite to the dark rock that is called the Blind Cow. The golden sun, yielding to the sea and land the last hot kiss of such a long spell of pleasant weather, caused the little waves to dance and to shine.

Under the Blind Cow the waters were dyed black by its heavy shadow, and to the blackness there Mary's imagination went. The waves splashed there, but not with the light of happiness. They curled with delight to murder, and seemed to watch Mary and to wait, the black rock jutting out and hanging over them, for her to come.

Mary stepped into the sea, and the waters reached to her knees, when she looked up and saw, very much to her horror—for death himself would be wearing a shroud—a naked man, the Nellie-bird, standing upon the rock.

When one has decided to end it all, one certainly wouldn't be expected to be over modest about any nakedness that may be met with in going down to those black waters.

But there is all the difference in the world between most of us who live in towns, and the other Mary who lived in Mockery Gap.

Although she had known rather more about Simon Cheney than is proper for any young lady who isn't married, yet between him with his clothes on and the tall shining body of the naked fisherman there was a vast difference.

The sun, who appeared to be less astonished than Mary, set a burning and a shining match to the fisherman's hair, that seemed at that moment to be on fire; while his limbs, white and still glistening with drops from the sea, appeared to belong, by reason of their perfect proportion, to some high spirit from above rather than to a plain, though unnamed, fisherman from those islands.

The man appeared by his gestures to be casting an invisible net over the girl.

It is possible to be awakened from the very saddest state of mind by a sudden burst of colour. A colour that burns can do more than make us merely happy: it can give us life.

The light that lightens the world can shine in a daisy; it can also shine in the human form when it is naked and fair.

But although Mary was saved, her 'Oh!' of astonishment wasn't in the least an exclamation of admiration, but rather the cry of a child when she sees something that she doesn't quite know the use of, a snake or a toad.

Seeing her there, and hearing her word of astonishment, the fisherman, who had only expected to see a barren shore when he climbed up the rock upon the other side, dived again and swam out to sea where his boat was anchored.

When Mary turned, she saw that her father's cows, driven there by the flies, had come down to the sea too, as if they wished to know what their mistress was doing. While behind them at a little distance she found her father, who was studying his map, the present from Mr. James Tarr.

Mary helped her father to drive up the cows. 'She was forced,' she said, 'to go into the sea after them.'

"Twould be nice,' said Mr. Gulliver to Mary, as they walked slowly up the green lane behind the six cows—"twould be nice for I to see with me woon eyes one of they little mermaidens.'

'But they bain't all wi' fishes' tails,' said Mary.

'No,' replied her father, 'there be those that some do call sirens.'

'Wi' legs same as ours be, grow'd.'

'You've been studying the world too,' said Mr. Gulliver proudly.

"Twould be nice,' said the farmer again, going back to his first thought. 'If one of they sirens would come to we, 'twould be something for wold Caddy to tell ducks about, for 'e do say they won't lay if they bain't told nothing.'

Mr. Gulliver put his arm round Mary and kissed her cheek.

'I begin to wonder,' he said, 'if it so happened that a siren did come to we, could 'e grow like a human and call I "grandfer"?'

"Tis all done wi' learning,' replied Mary decidedly. 'You've only to call out "grandfer" loud enough and they'll speak it.'

'What do a siren eat?' inquired Mr. Gulliver; 'they bain't like stoats, be they, that do eat rabbits?'

'I'll ask Mr. Caddy,' said Mary, blushing.

The cows walked slowly; the evening gnats played about them in the still, sleepy air. And the fisherman, clothed now, sat beside his boat and mended his nets.

Chapter 30

MR. RODDY SETS OUT FOR
A SAIL

SQUIRE RODDY, the far-famed discoverer of the little shells named Roddites, lived at High Hall, near Weyminster.

He possessed a collection of ancient monsters that with immense care and skill he had dug out of the earth, with the assistance of his three gardeners.

Besides the monsters, that Mr. Gulliver would certainly have recognised as being near of kin to those portrayed in his map, Mr. Roddy had scattered in his front drive so many of the little shells, that have brought him so much honour, that he was saved the trouble and expense of buying gravel.

When any visitor to Mr. Roddy's mansion had walked about until he almost wished the Roddites on the downs again and the monsters in the clay, Mr. Roddy would show him, who would fain have an easy-chair and something nice to drink, the very earthenware pot in which the poison had been placed that took the life away, beginning with his feet first, of the wise Socrates.

The visitor, after having looked so long and stared so hard, often wished that the cup were full.

Although Mr. Roddy's estate was a pretty

good one, for nearly all Mockery Gap was his, yet if anything happened to be given away in the neighbourhood of Weyminster, such as a free gift of the greenest and most succulent of turnip tops, that a farmer might well wish to have removed, for fear his lambs should scour, Mr. Roddy would send his men to collect some sacksful for consumption in High Hall, or else to use in the garden as manure.

Amongst his other worldly possessions, Mr. Roddy owned a small yacht, and sometimes he would sail in it a little way, and visit any little cove where a new fossil might perhaps be discovered that he could give a new name to.

Mr. Roddy's wife, a gentle and amiable creature, had the wisdom when her husband went a-sailing to remain at home. For Mrs. Roddy feared that the new maid, culled from the workhouse, might in a fit of recklessness or fear cast out of the window the bones of some long-extinct monster, that would soon be trampled into the dust of the road.

But there was something besides stones that had always interested Mr. Roddy since the days when he was a little boy at school. This was a wreck at sea. Mr. Roddy had often dreamed that he was there upon the seashore to pick up what the sailors—a set of extravagant rascals—had cast overboard.

At breakfast one morning—the month of September was well in—Mr. Roddy read in

the *Times* that a small vessel had run in a fog
upon the Blind Cow Rock in the Mockery bay,
and that the captain had been obliged to cast
overboard some of the cargo, which consisted
of cases of tea; though he wished he hadn't,
for in a very little while after doing so the ship
was pulled off by the Weyminster tugboat.

As soon as Mr. Roddy read of this event, he
said to his wife: 'A case of that tea would be
just the thing for the servants.'

Mrs. Roddy smiled as sweetly as she always
did when he made any kind of suggestion, and
replied that she hoped the new maid would
work better for it.

'And if,' said Mr. Roddy, warming to the
pleasant theme, 'Miss Ogle were to call we
might give her some too; you can't imagine
how thirstily she always glares at the poison
jar.'

'I will invite my friends for a sail,' said
Mr. Roddy.

It was always a glad and happy day when the
field club, of which Miss Ogle had now become
a firm and established member, went upon its
expeditions, generally by car.

But sometimes—and this is what Mr. Roddy
now contemplated—a picked number of the
members would be asked to go for a sail in the
yacht. And so it now came about that Mr.
James Tarr, Miss Ogle, and Mr. Gollop were
invited by Mr. Roddy to take part in a sea trip

to discover the spilt cases of tea, or, if not that, at least to find a new hunting-ground for bones, so that when the other members came they would merely have to step right into a stratum of monsters as into another world.

When the day came, and the yacht was upon the point of starting, with Mr. Roddy at the tiller, and Mr. James Tarr, who alone understood and alone managed the sails, to deal with them as if they were window blinds—a packet of letters was thrust into the squire's hands by the little maid, who knew the way to the quay because the same road led to the workhouse.

These letters each bore an American stamp, and were addressed to J. Roddy, Esq., the famous discoverer of the Roddites.

Mr. Roddy looked proudly at the packet, but as it was important to catch the little wind that was blowing, in order to make way as fast as possible to Mockery bay, he thrust the letters into his pocket until a more suitable moment came to open them.

The start had already been delayed for some hours, because Mr. Gollop had a funeral to take at three; and so it was not until four in the afternoon that the boat got away from its moorings and sailed out into the bay.

It was then, with the yacht about the same distance from Mockery as from Weyminster, that the wind in a September fit of idleness entirely failed to blow. And it was only dis-

covered at this juncture that the oars, that right-
fully should have been there, had been taken
from the boat by some thief or other; so that,
as there was no wind at all, the yacht was now
entirely in the hands of the sea waves, at whose
mercy it was likely to remain for many an
hour.

Chapter 31

A BED OF WITHIES

THE Saturday before Mr. Roddy had invited his friends to go for a sail, the fisherman delivered a basket of fish, freshly caught, at the Mockery vicarage. Rebecca had taken them in, fried them for breakfast, and placed them upon the table, near a dish of tomatoes.

The fisherman had lingered for a few moments beside the garden gate, the small one by which Mr. Pattimore had stood when he heard the countrywomen talking.

Rebecca, looking out of the kitchen window, saw him there, and saw him make a gesture with his arms as if to cast a net over the vicarage.

When breakfast was ready and Mr. Pattimore had eaten of the fish, in a fit of absent-mindedness, really wishing to help himself to another without looking at his wife, he took the pepper-pot in his hand and going to the dining-room window he looked out. He saw the fisherman.

He came back to his chair again, put the pepper-pot down, but instead of helping himself to a fish from the sideboard he touched Mrs. Pattimore.

He leant over her and said, 'Nellie.'

Mrs. Pattimore started, her breath came and went in quick gasps, and she put her head back a little as if to receive a kiss that might be coming. But Mr. Pattimore caught the Dean's eye, and so, instead of kissing his wife, he helped himself to a fine tomato and ate of it, as though surprised that it wasn't a fish.

The following morning, before he opened his Bible, Mr. Pattimore put out his tongue at the Dean.

His text had been—and he was almost on the point of going to church—from Romans; but he now looked so hard at a verse in another book, that when in the pulpit the latter one was the only thing he could remember, and so he spoke these words: 'Come, my beloved, let us go forth into the field; let us lodge in the villages. Let us get up early to the vineyards; let us see if the vine flourish, whether the tender grape appear, and the pomegranates bud forth; there will I give thee my loves.'

Mrs. Pattimore hardly dared to lift her head all the while the sermon was being preached. And when at the last, after having described all the fair and pleasant ways of love, and going even so far as to commend all naked delights in grassy places, where the Church seeketh for its spouse and findeth her always willing to be loved, he concluded by saying:

'I rose up to open to my beloved; and my hands dropped with myrrh, and my fingers with sweet-smelling myrrh, upon the handles of the lock.'

As soon as ever the sermon was ended,

Mrs. Pottle, who happened to be in church, hurried down the aisle and went along the lane to find Mr. Caddy.

"Twouldn't be fit for they poor ducks to hear,' exclaimed Mrs. Pottle, 'so thee best let they swim in pond without repeating what I do tell 'ee. And what poor 'oman however wold will be safe in Mockery now parson do begin to talk?'

Mr. Caddy shook his head.

"Tis thik fisherman,' he said mournfully. 'An' 'tis a fine pity that postmaster didn't ride over 'e instead of killing poor Mrs. Topple in lane.'

'She never fell down from high bank, then?'

'No, no,' said Mr. Caddy, loud enough for the ducks to hear, 'Mrs. Topple were murdered....'

The excitement of preaching such a sermon carried Mr. Pattimore on with wide wings that even Mr. Tarr's Nellie-bird would not have despised. He was carried through the Sunday night in an ecstasy of longing and of love. He wanted to shout out 'Nellie!' to the fond stars that looked in upon him all that night.

On Monday he said very little, but whenever he looked at his wife, at meal times—and she couldn't help blushing when he looked—he saw her as a woman young and pleasing, with a woman's longing calling for a man all about her, and wishing so much, in every gesture that she made, to yield up all to him again, as she had yielded herself, more wickedly than Mr. Pattimore had then thought quite proper, in the hollow of the cliff.

She didn't look at him when she went upstairs to bed, but she did turn a little when she opened the door, with the candle in her hand, that gave a new loveliness to her body that appeared then to be panting with hope.

Mr. Pattimore would have taken her at that moment, as a lion a lamb, only he felt that other eyes were upon him—and he saw the Dean.

Dean Ashbourne looked as sternly as a dean who had taken three wives to his bed, and all merry ones, could look at any one who, like poor Mr. Pattimore, was hesitating on the brink of perdition.

Mr. Pattimore climbed the attic stairs as if the cold grey eyes were after him looking damnation.

But the very bed, alas!—as though it joined with the Song of Songs to prove that the Church was no better than she should be, or perhaps having wished to help Mr. Caddy to a story—proved to be harder than ever.

All the night long Mr. Pattimore tossed and groaned. He looked out at the stars, which during that mad Sunday night had reminded him, by shining so wantonly, of all that had happened after he touched her first in the green bush until that day when the cold, painted eyes—who had already begun to look at another maid when his second lady was in a consumption—told him that if he wished to attain to earthly glory and heavenly bliss he must take to himself, as another bride, hard chastity.

Mr. Pattimore sat up; his longing and excitement were become only pain.

There were no stars.

He threw back the bedclothes, and said 'Nellie!'

This was the second night that he had not slept, but now, having said 'Nellie,' he could stand the loneliness no more.

Mr. Pattimore descended the attic stairs.

The hall clock struck four.

He now stood like a thief upon the soft carpet of the landing where his wife's bedroom was.

He was a robber with a mind to steal his own back again; to steal the lamb with all the fury of those long years of abstinence from thieving; to steal her as a lion would steal. Mr. Pattimore's teeth chattered; he hadn't trembled so since he had stood naked beside all that soft whiteness that hid its eyes from seeing him upon the cliff.

But now he intended that all his anger, restraint, rage against the fisherman, hope of preferment, youth, age, hot summer and cold winter, should rend and tear her in the fierceness of his longing.

Mr. Pattimore held up his candle and looked at her bedroom door.

He hadn't expected to see it open; 'but perhaps,' he thought, 'she might have felt the late summer night a little close.'

Mr. Pattimore blew out his candle; he wished to take and eat all of her in the darkness.

He hadn't been into her room since he had looked for the kite and had received the shock of seeing that white frock again. He knew her night garment—for he had once helped her to choose one, such a dainty one!—would be as soft.

He felt the bed. It was empty. Mr. Pattimore found the matches and struck a light. Her bedclothes were turned back, and she was not there. Near to the pillow was the baby's gown that she had been sewing.

Mr. Pattimore's excitement was very great; he fancied for a moment, because he saw the very bed garment that he knew, that was thrown carelessly down, that she was gone out naked in the night to meet the fisherman.

But ideas and suspicions that are as wild as the wind and as unreasonable change quickly. And Mr. Pattimore now fancied—for he knew that since that day upon the hill she hadn't even spoken to the fisherman, except perhaps merely to inquire about the freshness of the

crabs that he sold—that she had gone down
before the dawn came to pray beside the
Dean's picture for her husband's necessary
salvation.

'She must be gone down to pray,' he said.

Mr. Pattimore returned to his attic. He
dressed himself slowly; there was no hurry,
he would dress himself quietly and go down to
her and join her in asking for strength. He
knew a kneeling woman in the cool dawn,
below the portrait of a man of God, couldn't
be a temptation. He would go to her and ask
to be forgiven for all the wicked thoughts of the
past two days.

But instead of going straight into the dining-
room, where he hoped to find her kneeling,
Mr. Pattimore went—for his other suspicion,
though he had put it behind him for a moment,
was wide enough awake—to see if the front
door, that he remembered fastening before he
went to bed, was still locked.

He found the door open.

'The fisherman!' gasped Mr. Pattimore.
'The Nellie-bird!—and I might have been
loving her for all these years! Damnation
seize Dean Ashbourne!'

Wishing perhaps to hurry on with, or at
least to illustrate, the most sensible way that
God could deal with him when He got hold of
the Dean, Mr. Pattimore, choosing an oak
stick that he used when walking, entered the

dining-room and struck the portrait full in the face. The glass was shivered to atoms, and the picture fell with a loud crash.

'It was all owing to you,' shouted Mr. Pattimore, 'that I ever left my Nellie!'

Mr. Pattimore leant over the table and wept.

'Of course, how could he have expected her, a woman who liked love, and who must have always been thinking of it even when she dreamed of a frog in the green bush—how could he have expected her who lived so longingly, and sewed all her hopes into tiny garments with tiny stitches, to live for ever without a companion to console her heart and to breathe together, with her breath and his, in the net of love?' But then—and rage stayed his tears—how could she have left even his cold-heartedness that had called her Dorcas, to go out to one who did little more than idle about the village lanes in the hot sunshine?

Mr. Pattimore held his stick firmly and went out of the front door.

It was the hour before dawn, and a warm fog like the softest woollen blanket covered Mockery.

Mr. Pattimore stood for a moment and listened, and a muffled sound, dulled and softened by the fog, came to him—the breaking of the waves of the sea.

Mr. Pattimore strode down the lane, feeling his way cautiously, and, finding by good luck the stile, he climbed into Mr. Gulliver's meadow.

The first thing he did there, still following the sound, was to fall over one of Mr. Gulliver's cows.

The cow rose, and Mr. Pattimore, though a little unsteadied by the encounter, went on.

Mr. Pattimore was now aware that something else, some other sound, soft and consciously human, came to him as well as the splash of the waves.

In the tiny copse of withy bushes that grew near to the sea some one was sobbing.

Mr. Pattimore had always been interested in these beds of withy that grew so near to the shore. He had fancied once that the willow should only grow in marshy places inland where baskets were made.

He now remembered noticing that the new fisherman was one day busy making a lobster-pot, and so he supposed that his wife was with the man there, who, early astir, had gone to the copse for wood.

Only a few days ago he had heard of a legend that told how Jesus had been whipped with a withy by His mother's aunt, an old lady who used to say there was no good in the boy, and so the willow always grew in watery places because Jesus shed tears when He was whipped. And in Mockery, as affirmed by Mrs. Pottle, and proved sometimes too, a maid or wife who wasn't loved would go down to the withy bed to cry, feeling, perhaps, that love, acting this time as an old aunt instead of a pretty boy, was whipping her so that she had to weep too as Jesus had done.

Mr. Pattimore found her there, but alone; and after he had kissed her tears away, exactly as the aunt, who really was very fond of Him, did those of Jesus, and called her Nellie, three times, he bethought him that he had been unjust to the fisherman.

'You only came here to cry,' he said.

'I couldn't sleep,' she answered. 'The night was so warm and I was unhappy, because after hearing you preach the sermon I hoped for so many things.'

'We will find the Nellie-bird,' said Mr. Pattimore.

She clung to him in the mist, and they found their way out of the copse and to the sands, where they nearly walked into the fisherman, who was standing, in one of his sad moods, and watching the waves.

'You are going to fish?' inquired Mr. Pattimore, who, as he had risen so early, was beginning to feel in want of some food.

The fisherman stretched out his hand and pointed to a dim light that appeared to be just visible out at sea.

'I wish to beg your pardon,' said Mr. Pattimore, and would have said more, only a crash interrupted him.

After the crash there was silence again, except that through the dense fog, and from the direction of the Blind Cow Rock, a surprised voice came that said: 'If only I had given the candle to Miss Ogle to hold, instead of taking it to read my letters with, she would have seen the rock and we shouldn't have run into it.'

At the same moment that the crash came, a wind that arrived with the first light of day drove the mist off, and the Blind Cow Rock was plainly visible, though no boat nor any sign of life was to be seen.

Chapter 32

MR. RODDY LOSES HIS LETTERS

IT was fortunate for those who were clinging to the jagged edges, covered with slippery sea-weed, of the Blind Cow Rock that the fisherman had his boat near.

And as there was now light enough for the man to see what to do, very little time had run through the great glass before the fisherman had his boat beside the rock.

He found there, holding on as best they could—each one for himself—Mr. James Tarr, Miss Ogle, and the Reverend Mr. Gollop; but Mr. Roddy was nowhere to be seen.

When he had helped the saved ones carefully into the boat, the fisherman searched the sea in the near neighbourhood of the rock for Mr. Roddy, who, Miss Ogle was good enough to say, apparently knowing that nature abhors a vacuum, 'must be somewhere.'

The fisherman rowed round the rock three times, and then landed those whom he had saved, who were welcomed in a proper manner by Mr. and Mrs. Pattimore.

The fisherman had leaped from his boat and was looking intently at the sea, when a cry came from the rock, and he, evidently thinking that Mr. Roddy might drown before the boat reached him, sprang into the sea and swam in the direction from whence the cry for help had come.

When he was gone out of sight, for he dived as soon as he reached the rock, Mr. Pattimore, with the aid of Mr. Gollop—Mr. James Tarr was too interested in a little bone that he had found upon the beach to pay any heed to what was happening—got the boat afloat again and soon came to the rock, where they found Mr. Roddy upon it, he having climbed up out of the sea when the fisherman dived to look for him. When he was safe ashore, Mr. Roddy explained that as the boat disappeared he had found himself holding to the rock, but, realising that he had dropped his letters, he let go in the hopes of finding them, and, the tide taking him some distance away, it was some while, although he was a good swimmer, before he could reach the rock again.

It was Mrs. Pattimore who, when the company were safely warming themselves before the kitchen fire at Mockery vicarage, remembered the fisherman.

'No doubt he is still looking for Mr. Roddy,' suggested Mr. James Tarr.

'Or else he may be looking for my letters,' said Mr. Roddy, politely moving to one side so that Miss Ogle might dry her stockings.

'We had better all go to bed,' said Miss Ogle a 'while our clothes are drying.'

'Is there any one in Mockery who can carry a letter?' asked Mr. Roddy.

'There is Pring,' replied Mr. Pattimore.

Mr. Pring, discovered at once by Rebecca, for he was mending the road exactly outside the vicarage gate, readily—and how could such a fine letter-bearer refuse such a request?—agreed to carry the letter to Weyminster and deliver it safely at High Hall before breakfast.

That matter settled, Mr. Roddy and Mr. Gollop were shown to the spare bedroom, and Miss Ogle was taken by Mrs. Pattimore to her own room, where she was left to enjoy some hours of gracious sleep in the softest of beds.

Mrs. Pattimore, having arranged her guests so that they might receive the proper and fitting repose that they needed after such long hours of exposure, stood for a little while wondering where she had better go to obtain the repose that she too, after her tiring night, wished to have.

She waited for a moment uncertain, until Mr. Pattimore, to whom Rebecca had been explaining that a death was sure to follow the fall of the picture, joined her.

'There is the attic,' said Mr. Pattimore.

She allowed herself to be led there. Mr. Pattimore, who didn't seem to notice the hard lumps now, watched her—himself undressed and in bed—brushing her hair before the cracked looking-glass.

Once before he had seen her lips look as red, and all of her—all made, and for one thought alone—love for him.

She looked like a woman. Mr. Pattimore sat up in bed and watched her.

She had been but a girl when, in that white frock, with her hands over her eyes to hide those blushes, she had watched him. All her fine figure—for now she had begun to plait her hair—made Mr. Pattimore wonder how it could ever have been possible for him to desert such a garden of cherries, with its soft mounds and moss flowers, all those years when he had followed the advice of the Dean.

It was this unnamed and most likely drowned fisherman who had brought him to her again. 'The Nellie-bird,' said Mr. Pattimore aloud.

He couldn't resist an immediate desire to fondle her a little as she stood there before the glass, and to kiss her neck and throat.

Which treatment, though it did not help her much in the doing of her hair, Mrs. Pattimore only very mildly resisted, bidding him only be a little careful about a pin that she believed she might have used when she dressed so hurriedly in the night.

But what she liked better than this little rudeness was the name, that would always be hers now, that he whispered to her before they both fell asleep.

Chapter 33

SUNDAY TROUSERS

BREAKFAST was certainly taken late at the Mockery vicarage after the arrival of the wrecked visitors.

For it was not until three o'clock in the afternoon that those who had arrived so early were downstairs and happily eating.

Mrs. Pattimore, who looked a glad bride of twenty, helped the fish; for Rebecca had bought and carefully cracked the legs of—and how she got them no one inquired—some fresh lobsters, that Mr. Tarr found so much to his taste that he ate three of them, and even Miss Ogle didn't do amiss.

After this breakfast, no answer having come to Mr. Roddy's letter asking his wife to send a car for them, Mr. Tarr suggested a walk, as he hoped to see the effect of the seeds he had sown—seeds to rouse the people of Mockery from the sad mud of their own thoughts to an imaginative and exciting life.

Mr. and Mrs. Pattimore asked to be excused, Mr. Pattimore remarking that he was going to make a bonfire of the portrait of a man that had happened to fall in the night, and whom he couldn't bear to look at again because he was so disfigured.

'I wonder where Mrs. Pattimore slept?'

Miss Ogle inquired of Mr. Gollop, with whom she walked.

'Perhaps with the servant,' said Mr. Gollop innocently.

Miss Ogle looked at him sharply.

'I don't believe it,' she said.

Mr. James Tarr was by nature, as we have remarked before, inquisitive; he wished to see what had happened in the village since he was there last, and so he went into the churchyard.

Mr. Roddy too stepped briskly, followed by the others, through the gate; he hoped to find some Roddites there, but could only see gravestones, green grass, and yellow hawkweed.

Mr. James Tarr stood, his face reddened with the hot summer, and his strong square figure very much alive, beside Miss Pink's grave, that was pointed out to the visitors by Mr. Pring the messenger, who, when Mr. Roddy asked if the car would come, replied that he never lost a letter.

'An' I've had me dinner,' said Mr. Pring, who had been trimming the hedge.

Near to Miss Pink's last resting-place there was the grave of Mrs. Moggs, and a little further away Mrs. Topple was laid to rest— dying, so Mr. Pring informed Mr. Tarr, as if to remind that gentleman of his own good advice, 'by means of a clover leaf.'

Mr. James Tarr had expected, as every one does, to find some new graves, perhaps two or three, in a country churchyard, as well as the old ones.

'And how did Mrs. Moggs come to die?' asked Mr. Tarr.

''Twere the mice,' replied the roadman, 'that drowned she.'

Upon Miss Pink's grave Mr. Roddy now noticed an oddly-shaped stone, that he took up in order to examine more closely. On lifting the stone he discovered a letter underneath it, the very letter that he had handed to Mr. Pring to take to Weyminster.

All the company looked at Mr. Pring, who in his turn looked at his own trousers.

'They be me Sunday ones,' said Mr. Pring, 'for t' others be broke, an' there bain't no pocket in these.'

'T' other letter,' he said, 'that Miss Pink did give to I for wold Gulliver, I did hand back to she again, for I did put en in grave; but thik'—and Mr. Pring held up Mr. Roddy's— 'I were only given this morning, and I don't never go nowhere only on Sundays.'

Mr. Roddy looked at Mr. Pring as if he were but another odd symbol, like the stone that had fallen from the church roof that he now held in his hand.

'You didn't think, did you,' inquired Mr. Roddy, addressing Mr. Pring, 'that I really meant you to carry away my letter and to hide it?'

'I be one,' said Mr. Pring proudly, 'who have never lost a letter, but t' other be thik that I've kept the longest. An' now 'tis buried, for Caddy do say that they grave beds be best and safest.'

'Mr. Caddy,' said Squire Roddy; 'I remember the name, for poor Pink paid Gulliver for his new gate, and I ought to show Miss Ogle how gates are made if she is to be agent here.'

Mr. Roddy and Mr. Tarr reached the hedge—through which the rude children had watched Esther—some while before Mr. Gollop and Miss Ogle had left the churchyard, for while waiting there they had decided to be married in four weeks' time.

Mr. Caddy was telling his ducks a story, and the squire and Mr. Tarr listened unnoticed.

''Tis best,' said Mr. Caddy, watching his ducks, who were fast asleep with their heads under their wings, 'to do nothing, only sleep.

'And there be a bed where nothing bain't done worser than thik.

'I did think,' said Mr. Caddy a little louder, 'that if Postmaster Hunt were hanged for murder 'twould be a punishment, but now I do wish 'e to live.

'A bed that be silent an' that don't never creak be too good for 'e.

'They ducks,' said Mr. Caddy, 'do bury their heads for to show we how best 'tis to lie; they don't listen to no Mr. Tarr nor to no

Squire Roddy when rent time do come. Miss Pink's bed be the best.'

Mr. Tarr whispered to Squire Roddy that perhaps, instead of waiting for Miss Ogle to come, they had better go and visit Farmer Gulliver.

Chapter 34

THE SIREN

Miss Ogle and Mr. Gollop were standing silent upon the Mockery green when Mr. Roddy and Mr. Tarr came to them. Mr. Gollop was looking at the cottage shadows in a meditative manner, and for a good reason, because he was calculating the exact sum that Miss Ogle would be likely to spend from her own money for scented soap and face powder.

The evening was still and sultry, and the shadows that Mr. Gollop was looking at were slowly lengthening. The Mockery meadows that reached to the sea were decorated with gossamer, created by billions of minute spiders, who for reasons of their own clothed the lovely maiden earth with a delicate garment.

The gossamer floated in the air and twined itself in silky ribbons about any who walked in the fields.

Mr. Gulliver's cottage, one of the prettiest in the village, stood a little way back from the lane.

A pleasant path led to it through a field now yellow with ragwort, while the cottage windows peeped from under the thatch and eyed the approaching visitors with inquisitive interest.

Coming nearer to Mr. Gulliver's, it was easy to see that something had happened that drew the attention of Mockery to the little cottage.

Here were all the Mockery children collected, who of late had become more modest, with the fisherman to play with, but were now, alas! behaving as the poor man did who took to himself seven devils instead of one.

The pack of little wolves, merry again in their old manner, were shouting out to each other that the other Mary had given birth to a monster with horns and a tail, and, indeed, the very beast that Miss Pink had at first been afraid of.

As soon as Mr. Roddy approached them, they ran further into the fields, kicking up their legs and making faces as if to show what the monster was like.

At the door of the cottage Mr. Tarr, who arrived the first, found Mr. Gulliver, who whispered to him in a voice of mystery that 'a siren had been discovered that very morning in bed with his daughter.'

After communicating this strange intelligence, Mr. Gulliver had at once gone upstairs, leaving Mrs. Pottle, who was clad in a matronly apron, to explain the matter further.

'Do 'ee come upstairs and see what 'tis,' said Mrs. Pottle, inviting Miss Ogle to follow Mr. Gulliver.

Miss Ogle went to the bedroom, but in a moment she returned again and invited her friends to ascend too to see the monster.

In a pretty bedroom, such an one as a

modest country-girl with a nice dislike of all that is naked would have to sleep in—with her dolls, that she still petted, with all their garments on, and the windows near hidden with curtains—they found the other Mary. She was in bed, a little pale, perhaps, but holding very near to her, and looking at it as only a mother can, a tiny creature with a fine show of hair, who was asleep and happy.

Near to Mary sat her father, who was regarding the little one who lay upon his daughter's breast with the rapt attention of one who views for the first time in his life something that is mentioned in a picture, but is to him entirely new and strange.

Mr. Gulliver now left his place beside her, and came to Mr. Roddy and whispered to him so that he wouldn't disturb the sleeping babe, but with all the excitement of one who has received what he wished for:

''Tis well 'tis only a siren, and not one of they fire-drakes, that be come to our Mary.'

'I should like,' Mr. Roddy whispered back in return, 'to be the siren's godfather.'

'And I will be her godmother,' said Miss Ogle.

Mr. Gollop frowned.

Returning to the green, Mr. Roddy and his friends found Mr. Pring, who was trimming the grassy sides and paused when they reached him to address the weather. 'I do know now

264

that she be a woman,' said Mr. Pring, 'who be good-tempered at night time. But 'tis in the morning that she do burst into a tempest and thunder and rain.'

Mr. Pring raised his hand and pointed to the sky.

'When thee do bide most quiet, wold 'oman,' he called out, 'thee be only breeding bad weather.'

Mr. Roddy and his friends moved away, but not so fast as to prevent them hearing Mr. Pring repeating over to himself that 'there wasn't any one in the whole world who could carry a letter or a message so carefully as he could.'

Mr. Roddy took tea at the vicarage, and was upon the point of settling an important matter, whether or no to return home in the most simple manner possible, that of walking there on his own legs, when Miss Ogle and Mr. Gollop came in to say that the ill-mannered children of Mockery had informed Rebecca that a large car had been seen upon the cliff.

This news had been communicated to Miss Ogle and Mr. Gollop, who were walking in the vicarage garden and talking about furniture in a manner that would have pleased Mr. Caddy.

Rebecca had heard the word they mentioned, and when she pointed out the car to Mr. Gollop she blushed prettily.

Mr. Gollop, who didn't seem to mind taking away another gentleman's maid, and as it wasn't in his nature to refuse a blush, at once invited Rebecca to come to them in a month's time, when they would be married.

Rebecca replied in a friendly manner that 'she would very much like to,' for ever since the portrait had fallen she had been most mournful. 'You will be a dean one day, I hope, Mr. Gollop,' she said, 'for deans are so knowing.'

Mr. Gollop smiled.

Miss Ogle frowned. But Rebecca, who thought a clergyman's smile who was rich enough to become high one day was something a great deal grander and better than the simple ways of a common fisherman, agreed willingly to go.

The car seen upon the cliff, the very same that appears at the beginning of our story, has now come to end it.

It had indeed taken but a few hours for the remaining members of the club, after the news that Mr. Roddy was wrecked at Mockery reached them—for all messages (and would that they were!) are not always handed to Mr. Pring to take care of—to assemble together and mount the car, hoping at least to find the bodies.

The gentleman and ladies, consisting for the most part of the very salt—or better still, pepper—of the earth, the county families,

had with them their umbrellas and overcoats
—for one old gentleman, who looked at the
weather just as queerly as Mr. Pring, expected a hard frost that evening; while a lady
believed a thunderstorm was brewing.

Mr. Roddy, who climbed the hill first, was
received with proper and fitting acclamations
of joy; and Mr. Tarr at once mounted the
tumulus and was about to commence a lecture
upon the exact shape of the concubine's earrings—that had never been found—when a
sad groan interrupted him, that appeared to
come from the very bottom of a deep hole that
was dug in the mound.

Mr. Tarr looked down into the hole, and
saw at the bottom Farmer Cheney himself, who
had spent all that summer in digging in the
mound for the earrings that, once discovered,
would bring him, he believed, enormous wealth
and, as Mrs. Cheney was always repeating,
would enable Master Simon to go out at night
time with real ladies instead of mere servant
maids whose clothes every one knew about.

And so here, this very afternoon, when he
began to descend into the hole, Mr. Cheney
had fallen, and had already lain for some hours
with a broken leg, with his skull beside another
human skull, though prehistoric, that he un-
earthed with his fall and which fell with him.

Mr. Tarr climbed into the pit and took the
older skull into his hands, telling Mr. Cheney

that he had made a most important discovery; and ascended to the mound again, where he explained to the company that the skull was the very thing that he had wanted so that he might complete his discourse about the earrings.

Mr. James Tarr was holding the skull in his hand, and was pointing out where the earrings should have been—for he believed the skull to be a woman's, and a naughty woman's, too—when Miss Ogle, whose rude manners knew no bounds, suggested that Mr. Cheney might be lifted into the car, laid at the bottom amongst the coats and umbrellas, and so be carried to the hospital.

Mr. Tarr watched this being done with the same expression of disgust that a preacher would wear who, enlarging upon his theme, 'that there is no such thing as death, and that only the most stupid believe there is,' sees at his very feet one of his hearers die of heart failure, and is obliged to wait until the corpse is carried off before he can expose the fallacy any further.

Mr. Cheney safely laid in the car, Mr. Tarr was beginning again, though in a louder tone, because Mr. Roddy had three times set foot upon the mound as though meaning to begin to talk too, when the rude Mockery children, who had climbed the hill to see the car depart, raised a sudden cry that something was moving in the bushes.

"'Tis what Mr. Caddy do tell of what they be doing,' shouted the children, who gave place to the ladies, who crowded to look too, but were, alas! only in time to see God Simon and Dinah Pottle rising from the mossy ground and crawling out from under the gorse.

Miss Ogle, the first lady to arrive, helped to arrange the blushing Dinah a little more properly, and to do up her hair that was fallen down; while Mr. Roddy, who was a just as well as a wise magistrate, commanded Simon to have his and Dinah's banns published the very next Sunday, or else to incur his anger.

The car was now ready for departure, while the sun, like the fiery head of a huge giant, was about to sink into the sea.

The car was turned, but it couldn't at that moment take the road, because a farm cart was passing.

In the cart there was a weeping girl, Esther Pottle, and the fisherman—the Nellie-bird.

The fisherman was now leaving the village with the few goods that he possessed, and was returning to those same islands from whence he came. He was not drowned. He had merely swum across the bay, when he knew Mr. Roddy was safe, and entered his hut unobserved; and that same day, feeling that fishing at Mockery could never be really a success, he decided to leave the hamlet.

The fisherman now kissed Esther, and told

her to dismount, for he couldn't take her to his home then, but promised, kissing her lips again, to send for her later.

As soon as the fisherman had gone over the hill, never looking back at the girl, the car proceeded on its way too, while the children of Mockery Gap shouted after Esther Pottle, who hurried home:

'The Nellie-bird! the Nellie-bird!'

But Esther, who was near caught up by the rude children, was lucky enough to come upon Mrs. Pottle, who was beating the bushes in the lane and scattering the leaves, and at the same time was shouting out that she wished the leaves were so many Prings, because she had quarrelled with her neighbour again now that the fisherman was gone, and with him the chance of buying cheap mackerel.